Coach's Hue

This story is meant for all coaches, but it is dedicated to my brother Rob.

By: David W. Piazza

Chapter 1:

Life is a great spectacle. Every individual's story is special in some aspect, but rarely is that story about a natural liberator. The fetus that would sprout to be known as Coach has been in the womb, cooking for over eight months now; he was due to be birthed on April 20th, 1998. On a late March day, however, Coach was just extra cargo during his parents' picnic in the Great Smoky Mountains when a rare incident transpired.

The day began like any other day. Coffee, and the smell of butter melting, permeated the two-bedroom ranch stationed in Eastern Tennessee. Denise and Jorge Morales were silently going about their routines on an early Saturday morning. Their plan today involved a short getaway where they would be able to enjoy nature and one another, peacefully. Things had finally seemed to settle for the young couple, and they both felt as prepared as any young parents can for their first child. Denise had been meticulously reading all the baby books and making all the changes in life. Jorge had settled into his job as a professional pornography editor, something that he and Denise had countless arguments about. It was not considered the noblest of professions. Jorge saw potential in the industry's future, and well, he was exceptional at what he did. The Morales's were ultimately honest and good Samaritans. Jorge did well enough managing the porn studio, and Denise worked from home promoting Jorge's new line of sex toys he had coming to market; That is the primary component of this celebratory getaway. They had a baby on the way, a steady income, and a prospective new business. The Morales's were emulating the American dream.

The car was loaded with all the essentials, beach chairs, blankets, wine, and charcuterie. The fine young couple embarked on their two-hour drive to the mountains with mostly content in their hearts.

The Morales's had not even left the neighborhood before Jorge started in on business. "Hey D, how has the promoting been for the 'love you two times' toys?" an excited gaze in his eyes and smirk upon his face.

Denise irritably replied, "I am trying my best, dammit, Jorge!"

Tears swelled in her eyes. What had started as a calm and happy morning, abruptly turned into a whirlwind of conflicting emotions. Jorge had not intended to spur up such emotions, but he knew how Denise felt about being involved in the porn industry, in any capacity.

Jorge concernedly glanced away from the road to meet Denise's eye. He stated, "My Sweet D, I know how you feel about what I have invested my life and efforts into. But people need love and satisfaction. Even if they have to give it to themselves."

Denise continued sobbing for ten minutes, and nothing Jorge could say seemed to quell her sadness. So, Jorge just reached out and held Denise's hand for the next 45 minutes in silence. Except it was not silent because Freddie Mercury subtly belted his new wave, melismatic tunes through the car speakers. Denise and Jorge mutually loved Queen, both because of the band's astonishing rise to stardom and the fated connection they helped foster between the couple. The Morales fusion took place at a Queen concert in Memphis in 1981. Jorge and Denise were both living lives even further on the liberal side of the spectrum. Jorge, with his thick and rugged mustache, protruding from his tan face, leaned in to drop a juicy line in Denise's unsuspecting ear.

"From where I am standing, I would say that you're the reason this rockin' world goes 'round."

Denise turned to see a fit young man with long dark hair, and an exceptional mustache, grinning from ear to ear. She knew Queen's material enough to know he was referring to her bottom. An awkward and silent five seconds had passed while Denise was considering how to respond. Her initial instincts had Denise yearning to throw the rest of her warm beer directly unto that burly mustache and focus back in on the show. But there was something about this young man that intrigued her in ways that no other had before.

Thus, Denise smiled and proclaimed, "damn right!" instead.

These two love birds shared a cozy smile and a deep stare before exchanging pager numbers and getting swallowed up by the crowd again. The encounter was short, but long enough to connect. That was the most critical factor. The rest was history, a beautiful and juvenile history.

Fast forward seventeen years, and we find ourselves eastbound on a Tennessee highway. The year is 1998, and the charming Morales couple are driving in a green Ford Explorer. Denise and Jorge just had a rendition of a 'fight' in which minimal words were exchanged, and no love was lost. They were still an hour away from their destination, and Queen's Greatest Hits album had begun its second revolution through. As 'Fat Bottomed Girls' started up through the speakers for the second round. Denise was quickly transported to that special event where she met Jorge for the first time.

After over forty-five minutes of silence, Denise whispered, "Hey, do you remember the importance of this song?"

Jorge, with his abstract sense of humor, played dumb to the question and quizzically glanced back at Denise and replied, "Absolutely, Queen is a legendary band."

Denise's face read of concern and disheartenment. She felt like crying again. But when she looked up, she saw that renowned ear to ear grin on Jorge's face.

Jorge quickly retorted, "Of course I do, Sweet Baby. This song means the world to me. Without it, without Queen, without fat bottom girls... I would be without you."

Denise's heart warmed. Her face turned red, her eyes watery, and she knew it too. 'Fat bottom girls make the rockin' world go 'round.'

Denise gathered herself after a minute and, with much relief, sighed and declared, "I am just feeling incredibly vulnerable during this last part of the pregnancy. I know that you provide for our family and me. I know that people are sexual creatures. I know that you are good at what you do. I love you, Jorge."

Jorge replied speedily, "I love you too, D."

Little more was said or needed to be said between the two lovers, but their aura was back on track. After a full two revolutions through the

Greatest Hits' album, Jorge popped in a Rolling Stones album to carry them over to their destination. The sun was peeking through a thinly clouded sky, and the high temperature on the day was to be 52 degrees in the area they normally frequented in the park. But today, Mother Nature would provide the Morales's with a different experience.

As they drove through the mountains and passed their usual departure point, Denise spouted, "Hey! Isn't that our exit?"

Jorge replied, "It sure is, D. But we are heading to uncharted territory today!" Jorge was excited and curious himself. Uncertain as to where they were being subliminally directed.

Excited, confused, and overwhelmed, Denise felt a lavish rush of emotions. She, like Jorge, always had an adventurous side.

Denise exuberantly announced, "I have been longing for some adventure! I can't wait to see what you have in store!"

Jorge smiled the entire ride down the mountain until they made it to a breathtaking place called Coach's Valley. Perplexed, Jorge did not recognize this name from any map he has studied. But the natural landscape they encountered instantly superseded any doubt they were in the wrong spot. The Morales's were both in awe as they spectated upon lush greenery, teaming canopies, towering ferns, and complex grasses at the base of the mountain. They both had tears forming in their eyes as they got out of the car and rotated around 360 degrees. It was their best effort to absorb all this natural glory.

"It is marvelous, Jorge! I have never seen anything quite like it!" shouted Denise.

Jorge was awestruck and speechless for the time being. This was not where he planned to venture to, and Jorge could not find this special place on any map he brought with them. But instead of worrying, Jorge just soaked in the moments of pure bliss with his lovely wife as the elated couple relished in the stunning environment where they found themselves. Jorge observed their surroundings more closely. He noticed that the road they drove in on seemed completely different than when they first arrived fifteen minutes ago. A mere shred of skepticism pierced Jorge's neck for a moment, but it was quickly washed away by the sight of tremendous splendor.

Denise was giddy, "Can we hike into this wonderland, Jorge?!? Can we please?!"

Jorge was excited to see his wife, so thrilled. Nothing else mattered at this moment. He enthusiastically responded, "Absolutely, My Dear. Let me pull the car up a bit so we can unload the supplies for the expedition."

Jorge did just that. Mr. Morales pulled up the road to turn the car around and back into the valley. He swore that the street had altered again in this short time they had been in Coach's Valley. "Maybe it seemed shorter, yet further away? Maybe the curvature had switched sides? Maybe less of the road seemed visible and more engulfed in the foliage?" Jorge could not be certain as he reeled off questions in his head. But what he was certain about was this was a magical place, and his wife was the most exuberant he had seen her in over two years.

As Jorge got the Explorer repositioned in the valley's landing, he exited the car and asked, "Hey Babe, do you notice anything different about..."

While formulating this statement, Jorge looked up and saw his eight-month pregnant wife dancing and twirling. Denise frolicked along the perimeter of dense vegetation with her hands out and her smile in full bloom.

Denise heard Jorge in the distance, and halted her dancing to respond, "What's up, Jorge!?"

Jorge worried about deviating from this instantaneous and magnificent ambiance they stumbled unto and replied with, "All good!"

As Jorge unpacked the car and loaded his person with all that he could carry for the hike, he took one more glance back at the road. Although they seemed to have only briefly started their walk into the forestry, it appeared as though the road was almost unidentifiable. "Perhaps all the fresh air was making these illusions seem more poignant than they are." Jorge consoled himself in thought. Whatever the case may be, the Morales's had found themselves in what felt like untapped Earth.

"How have we never been here before?!" proclaimed Denise as it seemed like she would never blink her eyes again.

"I wanted this to be a special trip for us and our little one. In honor of the creation of one more Morales," explained Jorge, half-clarifying his way through that answer.

Denise stopped to catch up with Jorge and kissed his right cheek before squeezing him tight. She was content with her life and felt blessed to have someone as special as Jorge to share it with. They trekked for what felt like hours but was only thirty-five minutes according to Jorge's golden timepiece. Famished and fatigued, they found themselves in an arboreal area consisting of giant grasses and silky earth. The ground was flat and soft, the trees were swaying in the cool winter breeze, but the temperature in this valley was ten degrees warmer than the forecast. It was perfect.

"Let us set up shop here, D. You ready to get down on some grub?" Jorge asked with excitement.

"I would love nothing more" Denise responded.

The two lay their blanket as a base, put out their lovely spread, and feasted like royalty. They smiled, laughed, served one another samplings of cheeses and meats while Jorge guzzled sizeable cups full of Cabernet. Denise was being responsible and limited her consumption to one glass, although that was more than enough to get her buzzed. The atmosphere was so fresh and inviting, they felt only ease. The picnic took a romantic turn after their appetites were satiated. Jorge pulled out a pre-rolled marijuana cigarette of Lemon Haze to cleanse the pallet and finish a wonderful lunch. While puffing away on the joint, they lay gazing up at the forest canopy. Again, Denise being responsible, decided not to partake at first, though surrendered to one swift taste. She took a quick drag on the doobie, and the two continued to ride the waves of maximum euphoria. They laughed more and touched one another in ways they had not for some time. As the intimacy heightened, Jorge went to his bag and pulled out one of his prototypes. The 'love me two times' edition. He promptly convinced Denise they ought to try it out, for 'quality control' purposes. She was delighted and satisfied enough in her current state that she agreed with little convincing. The two made love passionately and 'more than two times' for the next hour, or at least what seemed like an hour...

Chapter 2:

"Wow, what an incredible day! We haven't had one like this in years, possibly ever," Denise reveled.

"It really has been phenomenal! There's something about the air out here; the scenery, the sounds, the sensations, it is intoxicating on a different level." Agreed Jorge.

"Hey, what time is it even?" questioned Denise.

Jorge pulled out his timepiece, and it was stuck at 1:35 pm. "Hmm, how odd," Jorge thought.

There was still illumination within the lush canopy they had been fornicating underneath. But it was impossible to tell if the sun was still out beyond the dense foliage.

"The sun had to be out, though. How else could it still be so bright in this forest?" Jorge continued to think to himself. He had not yet reached the point of panic, but he had allowed some worry to sink into his psyche.

Jorge finally responded to Denise's question, "My watch has seemed to stop working suddenly. Should we start making our way back to the car?"

The Morales's were struggling to come to after a long, post-sex nap. They both felt disoriented but immediately associated this with the weed and wine. Once Jorge got to his feet, he helped his pregnant wife up. Denise appeared to strain more than when they arrived and emerged from the ground, subtly fuller in size although Jorge would never divulge this observation to Denise.

Things had grown to be precarious in their predicament, both Jorge and Denise had felt this sensation. The extreme euphoria of the day's past events had washed away. They both gathered their belongings and tried to recalibrate their minds back to reality, but this felt like an impossibility. A fog was hovering around their heads; they simply could not shake it.

Jorge reached for the supplies lethargically, and asked Denise, "How are you feeling?"

Denise replied slowly, "I feel like... The baby is ready to burst out! And incredibly stoned still, what did you put in that joint?"

Jorge pondered on the answer before stating, "It was just herb, I feel it too. This is not any cannabis-induced haze. This is something different."

Denise felt flustered, and declared, "I don't care at this point, let's head back to the car. I am not feeling so hot."

After they had collected all their materials, or close enough to all the materials they brought, team Morales stumbled back on the path they believed would take them to the Explorer. They had been walking for fifteen minutes before Jorge realized they were making circles around the same area, observing their footprints in the soft earth. Jorge and Denise had rapidly found themselves in a dire situation after experiencing one of the best afternoons of their lives. Panic and fear had encapsulated the young couple now, and the mysterious haze of the day had continued to linger over each of them.

Denise winced and screamed in pain while trying to keep her balance, as Jorge's pace quickened. Jorge was torn between failing to figure out how to return to their vehicle and comforting Denise. Pure adrenaline was now being produced through the dread bubbling up from Jorge's core. The young porn editor felt sweat build upon his brow, and he could hear each swift heartbeat rumbling in his ears. The Morales's tried every new direction they could but repeatedly found themselves at the same origin point. The origin point where they had, just previously, shared these magical moments.

"Denise, I-I-I do not know what to do." Jorge vigorously stammered.

Denise could not respond. She was keeled over near the edge of the cleared area they repeatedly found themselves back at.

"Can you hear me, Denise? Tell me how you're doing. Tell me what to do!" Jorge's voice had risen an octave or two.

Denise finally caught her breath enough to utter a statement, "I think the baby is coming."

"But... how?" Jorge manically pondered, "How is this possible?" she minimally had another month before the baby was due.

As Jorge starred worriedly at his ailing wife, he detected the warm and salty flavor of his sweat, making its way into his mouth. After quickly licking the sweat away, Jorge felt his mustache curling well over his quivering lip. He then put his hands on his face to feel a full beard spread across it. A beard that connected to his untamed mustache. Jorge prided himself on his manicured facial hair, and the routine he consistently stuck to for his whole adult life. This day was no different. When he woke up this morning, Jorge shaved his face and trimmed his mustache, just like he had always done. He was sure of it. Yet, at this current point, he was not sure about anything anymore. The fog had remained in his worried mind, and all Jorge could do was watch his wife labor on the forest floor.

"Just breathe, Denise," was all he could think to say at the moment.

Denise certainly did that. She was forcefully huffing and puffing with her eyes closed and back against the trunk of a red spruce tree. Jorge had helped shift her over from the tall grasses for more support. This tree was exceptionally robust in comparison with the other plants. Its trunk was three times the width of all the other surrounding timber, and it seemed to tower over every other bit of vegetation in the vicinity. Jorge, now feeling disorientated, starred at this magical tree. Jorge wondered if it had been there when he and Denise arrived in this area for the picnic. "How could I have missed this?!" Jorge fervently asked himself, distracted in thought. All the other flora was of a similar species and rather uniform in size. But this tree seemed to be the one monstrous spruce amongst a sea of evergreen. Its pinecones were a deep crimson color, and the leaves were a vibrant purple. The bark almost had a glossy golden color to it, as if it were metallic. It was mesmerizing to look upon, and Jorge found himself locked into its mystic beauty.

He was returned to reality by a piercing shriek from his wife, followed by a "holy fuck!"

Denise's cargo pants were saturated because her water had just broken. She directed Jorge the best she could to disrobe her and prepare to retrieve their baby soon. Jorge did as instructed. He was beyond the point of comprehension regarding this extreme transition from the reality they knew before entering Coach's Valley. Now sweating profusely, Jorge felt his throat swell, and his hearing fade, while he was entranced by the golden spruce Denise was propped up against.

From what felt like miles away, through muffled ears, Jorge could hear his name being called.

"Jorge! Jorge! JORGE!!!" cried, Denise.

In a frenzied state, Denise shook and rocked against the spruce's trunk. She was attempting her best to birth this premature child. As she bumped the spruce behind her, Jorge kept his eyes fixed on the tree's regal stature. Jorge was engulfed by this natural wonder. He could not seem to redirect his attention to his struggling wife, who desperately needed his support. As the moments intensified, Denise unremittingly pushed and slammed against the tree's trunk. This continued for over ten minutes until Denise felt something fall from a branch and bounce near her swelling belly.

It was a pinecone, or what they thought was a pinecone at first. Not the same, deep crimson pinecone that seemed abundant amongst this unique spruce. This pinecone appeared more like a precious gem. It was turquoise in color and smooth in texture. It did not look like something grown from a tree, yet it had fallen from the very spruce they had found themselves up against. Both Jorge and Denise redirected their gazes at the 'gem-cone' that had bounced next to Denise and landed in the brush to her right. The color was illuminating through the dark green grasses. Time had stood still; Denise no longer felt pain, and Jorge no longer felt paralyzed.

As they were both now transfixed upon the turquoise luminescence, Denise murmured, moving nothing but her lips, "What is that?"

Neither of them had blinked in the twenty-five seconds since this unidentifiable object fell and landed within their gaze. Time had seized in this moment.

Jorge, still mesmerized by the gem, uttered, "I have no idea, but it is marvelous." Jorge now had a full beard, red and weary eyes, and that famously full smile across his disheveled face.

Denise could hear a different pitch in Jorge's voice and diverted her gaze unto her husband's crazed face. She similarly observed the moment. The atmosphere was still; there was silence all around them. Denise could not feel her baby progressing its way out of her uterus in this halted moment. She could only see a ravenous Jorge; his hunger was not for food, but rather for something magical. Finally, focusing in, Denise could hardly recognize Jorge anymore. He looked manic, sweaty, and barbaric. The only recognizable thing was that smile she fell in love with, and even that seemed tainted in this perilous instance.

"How had things crumpled so fast?" thought Denise. "I just can't grasp what is happening or how it is happening." Denise continued to ponder frantically.

Both individuals felt a pressure building internally; some gravitational pull was occurring. Once again, Denise involuntarily turned her head back towards the vibrant gem-cone. She could almost hear a snarling coming from Jorge and was now feeling frightened of her significant other. As the pressure became too intense, Denise noticed Jorge's clammy and dirty hands stretched out towards the gem-cone. He was gradually pressing towards this object with the demented and perpetual stare of a rapacious wolf. Denise feared what may come next; she did not know what this turquoise enigma could be capable of. Or why, as soon as it fell next to them, they both became transfixed on its allure, and everything else seemed to succumb. What she did know is that she did not want Jorge to be the one to discover. Jorge was slowly inching closer to the gem-cone, with his arms stretched out, now only five feet away.

Denise shouted in a wild panic, "Jorge, snap out of it! Please, come back to me!"

Jorge grunted something that sounded like, "I wish I could." His eyes still locked upon the gem-cone.

He said softly, "I love you, Sweet Baby." All while never breaking his momentum or line of sight on the exotic item.

As he made his final lunge to grasp the turquoise, Denise instinctually vaulted her pregnant body to intercept the impending connection. In doing so, Denise settled on top of the turquoise gem-cone. As she lay on her back, covering this radiant nugget, Denise felt an intense rush of pain flooding through her body. Her skin glistened with sweat, her eyes watered, saliva ran from both sides of her mouth, and blood came coursing from her ears. She could feel the gem-cone burning into the center of her back, melting into her being. Denise was excreting from every orifice in her body. She convulsed violently, during which Jorge snapped out of his stupor and quickly assessed the imminent danger his wife and child were in.

Jorge, now conscious again, screamed towards his wife, "Denise, what the fuck is happening!?"

Denise could no longer speak; her throat had collapsed. She could no longer see; her eyes had melted. She could barely hear with what was left of her perforated eardrums. But she had sense enough to know it was

Jorge. Denise's response was to reach towards her back to direct Jorge's attention. Jorge immediately turned Denise's vanishing body to its side to find the turquoise gem-cone had worked its way into her back and spine. Like a chocolate chip into a half-cooked pancake.

Jorge, petrified, cried and shouted, "No! No! No, please, God! NO!"

Without hesitation, Mr. Morales reached for the dwindling gem-cone in his beloved wife's back. With both sets of fingertips gripped on the bulging half of the gem-cone, Jorge felt the stone melding unto his hands. His wife was making gurgling noises as she continued to expel liquids on her side, her skin bubbled. Jorge's hands blended into Denise's back, and ultimately the gem-cone that partitioned their now intermingling bodies. Squeals of pain and distortion filled the air around the deteriorating couple. Jorge's body followed the same pattern as Denise's; they were both liquifying together. As their organs and fluids collapsed and ejected from their carcasses, their skin and bones turned into a thin turquoise paste.

After two minutes of decay, this lovely couple was turned into a pool of supernatural, turquoise liquid. What was left was a miraculously matured fetus, still in its amniotic sac. As it lay there, engulfed in its parents' collective puddle, the umbilical cord sat stretched out in the center of these fluids. The human pond of turquoise juices was saturated with Jorge and Denise's clothing. The puddle was not hot, as one might imagine after two bodies melting in on one another. Yet, gaseous steam was rising from the surface of the turquoise muck.

Thirty minutes had gone by before the fetus slightly moved around. The evolution in the sac persisted, and there was also movement on the forest floor where this turquoise puddle had once been two humans. As the puddle shrank, the fetus' sac expanded; he was absorbing this turquoise liquid through the umbilical cord. Larger and larger, the sac continued to grow, until the baby had transferred this colored matter into its resting place. The amniotic sac was now eight times as vast as its original form. Here, the fetus would stew for the next three days in a foul concoction of its parents' transformed substances.

Following three days of marinating, the fetus had developed into the size of a toddler and had consumed the dissolved turquoise matter. As the toddler had outgrown the container in which it was confined, it poked through the membrane to embrace the Earth's atmosphere. The baby boy was two feet tall and twenty-one pounds consisting of mostly his parents' fluids. He slithered around the patch of soft, green Earth where his parents unknowingly perished. There were reminisce of filthy clothing around, and what looked like the residuals of a scene from a horror film. The innocent toddler was already mobile and crawling around in its birthing place, Coach's Valley; his connected umbilical cord shriveled upon contact with the atmosphere. As the boy was getting acclimated to its surroundings and human life, he felt the primal sense of fear peaking in his brain. This fear caused him to let out a loud roar. Strangely, the area that had served as a place of great love, tragic death, and new life was encircled by tall grasses again. The magical forest site shifted formation as the days passed. However, there was one narrow and leveled path leading away from this bizarre locale.

After slowly crawling around the area for over an hour, the boy finally found this avenue of delicate Earth and intuitively crawled through it. The child was oblivious to what he was leaving behind, where he was, or even what he was. But something, perhaps even this strange land, was guiding this boy back to civilization. The forest floor was exceptionally soft and forgiving on the baby's new skin. His pace was slow but advanced for a newly born, infant-toddler. Abruptly, the boy found himself near the green

Ford Explorer that his father backed up from the adjacent road. The car had

a thin layer of grime covering it as if it had been sitting there for weeks. The

road was once again visible, although the youngster had no clue what he

was examining. Another surge of primal fear came rushing through the

boy's brain, and he let out a howl that reverberated for miles through the

Smoky Mountains.

Chapter 3:

In the distance, roughly a mile and a half away, an older man was

going about his daily hike through his numerous acres of land bordering the

national park. He heard a distressed shriek come barreling his way with

brute force. Immediately, his ears perked up, and he redirected his path

towards the menacing sounds of anguish in the distance. He took twenty

minutes to get in a position, on the side of the mountain, where he could

spot a green Ford Explorer parked in a curious valley. He removed his pair

of binoculars from the hiking pack and examined the valley where this

dusty car was stationed. To his utter surprise, he saw a naked toddler

aimlessly clambering around the base of the car.

"Well, I'll be damned," spurted the man. He promptly mapped his route to the helpless child and burst into action.

The trek took sixteen more minutes until the savior man, Roger, stumbled upon the child, car, and valley. His eyes were wide while in his state of sheer bewilderment, Roger had never seen a sight like this one.

"Hey there, lil' fella. What the heck ye doin' out here all alone?" Roger quizzically said.

He had his faculties and knew that the baby could not speak. But the boy stopped, sat, and starred up at Roger with a big grin on his face. Through all the fluctuations of emotions Roger was feeling, his heart was warmed by the smile of this unusual child.

Roger smiled back and continued speaking at the boy, "Where is ye ma 'n pa, Boy?"

Without the ability to communicate, the boy simply turned his head towards the mysterious forestry he had just crawled out of. But the path the boy traveled on was now gone. Only impassibly dense vegetation remained around the perimeter of Coach's Valley's landing. Roger scratched his head and attempted his best to gather twisted pieces of this extraordinary puzzle.

He went to the car and found that the driver's door was unlocked. Roger

propped open the door and rustled through the car's remains. It consisted

mostly of your classic vehicle accoutrements. He found traces of gum

wrappers, coins, a lighter, a Queen's Greatest Hits CD case, etc. When he

finally got to the glovebox, Roger found the registration for the car; it was

registered to a Jorge and Denise Morales.

"Reckon this must be ye momma 'n papa, eh, Boy?" blurted Roger.

Roger continued to ravage the car in hopes of finding more

information about Jorge and Denise, or possibly the baby. He,

unfortunately, could not. Roger was stunned in a flustered state until he

abruptly remembered the child was still on the forest floor. The boy had not

moved an inch; he was still sitting upright with a confused smile across his

innocent face. Roger did, however, find an extra blanket in the trunk of the

Explorer and wrapped the boy up in it. He was profoundly mystified by

what he had happened upon. The car had been scoured for signs of

evidence, clues, and information. Thus, Roger called out into the forest.

"Jorge! Denise!? I got ye baby boy here!" he shouted into the overgrown brush.

Only the sounds of nature responded. The swooshing from the swaying tree canopies, animals performing in the distance, and the sounds of gentle whistling from the dense grasses.

"Ain't this the most peculiar goddamn thing ye ever did see?" Roger asked himself.

Roger attempted to walk through the thick plant life in the direction the boy continued to look. He simply could not find any footing or subdue the sharp greenery to press onward.

Instead, Roger continued to call out the only two names he had come across, "Jorge! Denise!" again, nothing but the sounds of nature.

"Well, sun gone down soon... We best get to steppin', Youngin." Roger asserted, in a somber tone.

Roger took one more lap around the valley's landing and called out after the young Morales couple several more times. He read a sign stationed near the parked car reading, Coach's Valley.

"I have never heard such a place 'round these parts," Roger stated.

Roger had taken on enough mystery for today, and he grabbed the young boy for the return venture back to his home. He had become a man of solitude after his wife died in an unfortunate car accident, seven years prior. Roger was always a loving man until that point; he wanted kids but could never have them with his wife. Roger was angered by this but adored his wife fully and unconditionally. They had built themselves a nice little life on the outskirts of the Smoky Mountains. Roger constructed their house out of stone, and it is surrounded by thick woodlands. The house consists of two bedrooms (for their hopefully child), a small kitchen, one bathroom, and a living room that also functions as a dining room. He received over seventy-five acres of forest and mountain land from his deceased father's will when he was thirty-seven years young. Much of the land serves as a conservation for local wildlife. Roger had become quite the curmudgeon through his past experiences with grief, but underneath the cynical layers was a gentle heart.

As Roger started the hour-long hike back to his place, he looked down at the young boy and noticed that his smile had faded. The boy's eyelids were losing the battle of consciousness.

"Ye get ye some rest now, lil' fella. We will sort all this mess out soon." Whispered Roger, with a twinge of uncertainty in his calming voice.

Roger recounted the situation in his head as he found a trail back to his domicile. "How long had this lil' guy been out there on the forest floor? Where could his kin be? Was he abandoned? Had somethin' terrible happened to his family?" A plethora of questions flooded through Roger's spinning brain. The sun had begun its day's setting as Roger felt the familiarly relentless weight of sorrow and misery lifting from his strained heart. He had grown accustomed to his sardonic mindset, and dwelling in the past heartaches, that comprised his life. But just in the short trip back to his residence, he had felt the pressure of these encumbering feelings lift from his being. An exorcism so relieving, that Roger's whole body had severely tingled from head to toe. He felt lighter emotionally, physically, mentally, and spiritually, but he could not understand what the cause of such sensations was. Though, when Roger glanced down at the young boy, he saw a turquoise hue covering his infantile body.

"What in tarnish is happen' here?!" Squealed Roger, with exuberance in his voice.

They had made it back to Roger's property, and Ole Rog walked with an extra pep in his step.

"Boy, ye are somethin' special!" he decreed.

The sun was at the tail end of its setting, and the sky was plastered with an astonishing bevy of pastel colors. Roger had not recalled seeing a sky so beautiful in over seven years. Not since his wife, Judy, had passed. He stood humbly on the porch of his home with a foreign, and turquoise-hued, baby in his arms. Ole Rog sobbed openly while the sun finished its magnificent journey for the day.

After gathering himself, Roger said, "I reckon ye must be famished, Youngin. Let's see what Ole Rog can whip up for ye."

Uncertain as to what this mysterious baby boy ate, or what age exactly he was. Roger decided it was best to stick with mashed cuisines for now. He went on in the fridge and fetched whatever fruits and vegetables he could scrounge up. Ole Rog tossed the produce in his blender and pureed them until he was left with a greenish-orange slop. It was all either personally or locally grown vegetation, so Roger knew it was organic and wholesome. He poured a bowl's worth for the boy and one for himself. The boy sat on Roger's leg and excitedly took in every spoonful of the vegetable medley.

"Ooohhh, I see ye is one hungry boy!" Roger giggled. He could not seem to feed the boy fast enough.

"I don't know what ye done to me, Boy. But I have not felt such ease in years. Ye are a miracle." Roger announced.

"Tomorrow we shall search for ye family. I don't have much information to go off, but I do see an address on this here registration." Roger persisted in talking to the toddler and offering any reassurances he could.

The night had snuck up on the two, and Roger decided it was time for them both to get some shut-eye.

"C'mon now, Baby Boy." He said as he picked up the swaddled child. "Let us rest our weary heads 'fore we take on the trials and tribulations of morrow."

The boy had fallen asleep, almost directly after eating his vegetable slop. Roger was brushing his teeth and thinking through his plans for tomorrow's journey. He fell asleep with the boy in his arm and a blissful smile on his face.

Roger's eyes popped open in frantic haste before dawn. He had just had the most incredible dream. He quickly looked over to his side and saw the boy, realizing that it was not a dream.

"Sun come up soon, Youngin. We best get to it!" Roger stated.

He poured another bowl of the vegetable puree for the baby and made himself a bowl of porridge. The two sat at the table and ate breakfast. Roger exulted in assisting the boy with his consumption while he was wolfing down his oatmeal. Ole Rog was eager to figure out what had transpired the previous day.

"I can't keep callin' ye, Boy... Ye deserve better than that." Roger briefly stated as he scraped up the rest of the mush for the child.

"How 'bout I call you, Coach?" Roger asked while feeding the boy his last bite.

"Ye were found in 'Coach's Valley' down there. Ye done coached me some lessons I needed to learn. How 'bout it?" Roger questioned again.

As he asked a second time, Coach had a huge grin on his face, confirming his approval of the name.

"Aight then, Coach it is." Roger agreed.

Chapter 4:

The sun rose, and the day was anew. Roger packed up his truck. He drove a, more than slightly, rusted 1976 Chevy. Ole Rog did not know exactly where they were headed, but he had a basic idea of the neighborhood in which the address on the registration belonged. Without the proper seating for a toddler, Roger manifested a makeshift car seat out of blankets, pillows, and old plastic totes. Upon retrieving Coach from the house, Roger noticed he seemed more robust already. "Perhaps it was an illusion brought on through these recent, and wild, incidents combine with a lack of clarity," Roger thought.

"See what eatin' them vegetables do for ye, Coach?" Roger chuckled to himself while stretching to pick up what he remembered as a light toddler.

Roger strapped Coach into his pseudo kid's seat on the passenger side of the truck, and the two hit the road in search of Coach's parents or family. Roger had not left his compound for months but was feeling like a younger version of himself today. The car ride was to take roughly two and a half hours, according to Roger's estimate. The time flew by as Roger played joyful tunes, and whistled, like a contently unburdened man.

He turned to look at Coach and exclaimed, "Coach! I could have sworn ye was lookin' turquoise last night!"

Coach just sat there, smiling.

They approached the Eastern Tennessee region that Roger predicted the Morales's house would be in. As they neared the public, Roger asked a fellow civilian for help.

"Hey there! Ye wouldn't happen to know of a Jorge or Denise Morales in this here neighborhood, would' ya?" He politely asked a couple walking their dog on the sidewalk.

The couple stood still upon hearing those names, "Have you not seen the news?!"

Roger felt nervous, but he exclaimed, "I most certainly have not, what's the word?!"

They shouted back from the sidewalk, "They have been missing for days now! And that poor woman was eight months pregnant!" the couple shook their heads in disgrace.

Roger felt his stomach drop, but had to continue, "Do ye happen to know where they was livin'?"

"Just two blocks up yonder." The couple followed back with, whilst pointing in unison towards the direction Roger's truck was facing.

"Thank you kindly." Roger concluded the conversation, nodded his head in respect and slowly rolled up the rode in search of the Morales household.

The house was easy to find. There was yellow tape stretched across the estate, and the property looked desolate. Roger slowly crept his truck up to the residence and parked across the street.

"Well, Coach, this look like ye home is here." Roger acknowledged as he continued analyzing the property through his opened passenger window.

Roger decided to quickly get out of the car and walk up to the property to see if he could observe anything further. As he was making his way up the drive, a Tennessee state police car rushed onto the scene. The officer sprinted the car up, sirens blaring, and parked ten feet behind where Roger had made it along the driveway.

As the cop slowly exited the automobile, he shouted, "Hey, what are you doing on this property?! This is an active crime scene!"

Roger was startled, and unconsciously rose his hands up in the air while shouting back, "I was hopin' to speak with the owners! I reckon I found their car in the Smokies."

The cop took his hand off the handle of his gun, which was still holstered to his side, and he gingerly approached Roger.

"How do you reckon that?" the cop hollered.

"I found this here registration in it." Roger assured, as he slowly reached for the piece of paper and pulled it out of his back pocket.

"Sir, would you be able to show me where this car is located?" asked the cop, as he took the registration from Roger and glared up at him with a curious look on his face.

"Absolutely officer, I am just here to help. My name is Roger Brottle, and I live on up at the edge of the Smokies, and I stumbled upon an abandoned car... And a ba-" Roger tried to finish the statement about finding Coach before they were both interrupted by the cop's walkie.

"Copy that." The cop responded to the inquiry, then focused back in on Roger. "Sir, I am going to need you to show me where you found this car." Retorted the cop.

Roger decided not to reply any further than, "Yes, sir," or reiterate that last statement about the baby he found, who was now in his car across the street. He was not sure why he ultimately kept that information from the cop. But this whole scenario felt far too peculiar for him to divulge too much information until he learned more himself. "If Mrs. Morales was eight months pregnant then how could that be her kin?" Roger thought to himself, after allowing that tidbit of information he received from the passing couple to sink in. "If they ain't the parents, then who is?" he expanded further.

Roger, now perhaps even more bewildered than before he made the trip to this neighborhood, led the cop back towards his property and Coach's Valley. They took over two hours to reply to where Roger thought the car was perched in Coach's Valley. When they returned to the site, there was no Explorer to be found, and the terrain had modified to become impossibly thick. Roger parked his car off to the side of the road and was in complete awe as he got out to look around.

"I am certain that this here the spot I found the car," Roger asserted. He worried that he was losing his wits.

"Sir, what is this? What are we doing here?" The cop demanded as he caught up to where Roger was standing in the thick brush. He was growing frustrated with the situation and took a minute to assess Roger in his entirety. The old man had a thick grey beard, confusion in his eyes, and tattered clothing on his back.

"Where did you say you lived, Sir?" the cop asked, as his curiosity rose.

Roger could not answer at first as he was lost in a daze of incomprehension and surprise, but he stammered back, "Just around the bend there." Ole Rog pointed Northeast towards his property.

The cop had grown tired of Ole Rog and decided he should at least see that Roger makes his way back home to wherever he lives.

"There is nothing but densely intertwined vegetation. I don't see how a car could make its way in here." Announced the cop, in an increasingly agitated voice.

Roger continued to visually comb this area, in amazement, for any trace of its previous form. Even the sign that read, Coach's Valley, was wrapped up in vines and was indecipherable after this biological transformation. It was as if nature had just covered its tracks.

Now feeling disturbed, he mumbled back to the cop, "I suppose ye right." His head hung down in embarrassment and uncertainty. "This is where I done found the registration, though." He reassured the cop.

The day had phased its way into the late afternoon, and the cop had reached his limit. He would not feed into this senile old man's wild tales any longer. The police officer grabbed Roger's shoulder in an act of comfort. The policeman was now convinced this was all just some absurd story devised by a lonely geriatric.

"Let's get you home, Sir. Can you at least show me where it is you live?" the cop urged Roger to gather himself enough to find his way back home.

Roger was insulted by the condescending tone the cop had used with him but was too perplexed to fully acknowledge it. So, he just replied, "Sure."

Roger hopped in his truck to see a smiling Coach peacefully sitting to his right. The cop walked past Coach's window but was too busy shaking his head and reporting back to base to notice the boy in the passenger seat.

"Where did ye parents' car go, Coach?" Roger sighed to himself as he started up the Chevy to take them back to his stone house.

Roger drove back to his place, and the cop followed behind him. Ole Rog parked his truck next to the house where he liked it and kept Coach in the car for now. Roger figured to himself, "I prolly shouldn't stir things up any more than I already have with ole Johnny Law, he already skeptical of my intellect." But Roger felt better than he had in over a decade. His mind and soul possessed renewed eloquence since he found Coach. "Why would I go and let this here precious specimen be sullied by the foster care system?" Roger asked himself before departing from his truck.

"I am deeply sorry, Officer. I swear I came to cross that registration 'n the car just the other day." Roger repeated to the cop. "What do y'all know 'bout this Morales couple?"

The cop was still seated in his car with the window open. He was scoping out the property they drove up on and spouted, "We know they went somewhere, but none of their friends and family know exactly where." The officer was distracted by calls coming in on the radio and hastily asked Roger, "Are you going to be alright, Sir? Because I really must be getting back, duty calls."

Roger was dumbfounded at the cop's lack of interest and countered with, "I'm not sure if ye hearin' what I'm tellin' ye, Son. That couple could be out in this here forest somewheres." Ole Rog had grown mutually frustrated at the lack of connection he and the cop were having.

The officer smirked at the elderly man and confirmed, "I hear what you have said. I am taking it into consideration, and I will be taking this registration with me." The cop looked behind him to plot out his departure from Roger's property.

"So, what y'all goin' to do next? Send out the search team this' a way?!" Roger exclaimed as he stared at the young cop's disenchanted face. Roger could tell that the cop had given up on believing anything that he said had any credibility.

"I am going to go back and talk with the Chief to see how many units we can send out this way." The cop could hardly contain himself in this response. He was now convinced Roger was crazy and stumbled upon the registration in the Morales's neighborhood.

"I'm going to get right on it," the officer mocked, as he reversed the car off Roger's land. "Thank you for all you have done, Sir." The young patrolman chuckled to himself as he drove away with haste.

Roger stood in his rustic driveway, further befuddled by the day's transgressions, and shook his head. He let out a "dumb shit."

Roger snapped to and realized Coach was still in his truck, patiently waiting like the magical specimen he is. When Roger went to retrieve Coach, he saw the same delightful smile he commenced this day with. A day chalked full of disorientation and inconclusion. Ole Rog grabbed the boy and brought him in the house to fix him more of that vegetable slop they had left over in the fridge.

As Roger prepared a bowl, he said, "I am simply amazed at what come to light today, Coach. And I do not believe them damn cops is gonna do a damn thing for ye." He turned around to see that gentle smile, "But it don't phase ye none. Do it, Coach?"

The two sat together and ate dinner, Roger racked his brain about how to proceed from here. He wanted to help Coach find his home. Ole Rog wanted to make sure this sweet baby boy is taken care of. Roger did not have a phone, television, or any current technology. Ole Rog knew he would soon have to head back towards civilization again to contact the police and hopefully get ahold of a more reputable officer. Coach had urinated all over the blanket he had been wrapped up in for over a day now.

"Look like we ought to get ye some diapers and clothes as well." Roger verified, as he cleaned up Coach and found an old white tee shirt to drape over him for now.

Roger was fatigued from the fruitless efforts of the day, and he prepared himself for bed. Coach, looking more matured than he did yesterday, was yawning away in a horizontal position on the bed. Sleep took them both.

Chapter 5:

This March 18th day launched with the spirit of optimism. Coach had his pleasant smile, and Roger felt inspired by the child's presence. He noticed more hair on Coach's head and several new teeth forming in his adolescent mouth. Coach's shoulders had delicately widened, and his torso lengthened since yesterday. But Roger had just accepted these anomalies after the wacky past 48 hours. They had their breakfast together again and hit the road for more answers, and some proper clothing for Coach.

As they exited the department store with an array of multiple-sized attire and diapers, Roger noticed a pay phone from afar. He strolled over with a cart full of Coach and clothes. Ole Rog gave the police a call to settle this ordeal.

The phone rang twice before someone at the station picked up, "9-1-1, what is your emergency?"

"This is Roger Brottle, and I am callin' 'bout them Morales folk on the news." Roger explained to the officer.

"Ah, yes, Mr. Brottle. How can we help you today?" the correspondent offered.

"Nah, see, I am tryin' to help y'all out. I done found they car near my property in the Smokies. I reckon they may be stranded in the forestry somewheres." Roger replied.

The dispatcher, on the other side, claimed, "We heard all about it from our fellow officer. He assured us that everything was status quo where you showed him around."

Roger immediately grew frustrated, and fired back, "That simple son'bitch wouldn't listen to a word I had to say. He laughed at me and disrespected me on ma' property."

"Is this what you're calling about then, Sir? Would you like to file a complaint?" the officer labored to say with any enthusiasm.

"Hell nah, I want to help y'all find this young couple." Roger insisted.

In the background, Roger overheard someone say, "Is it that crazy old geezer?"

The officer on the line facetiously said, "We have the registration you found, that has helped us tremendously."

Roger felt his blood boil, yelling through the line, "What the hell wrong with y'all?! Do y'all police not wanna to do any goddamn police work, is that it?!" Roger had to breathe through the frustration. He continued before the officer could respond, "What have y'all done to find these folk? I am offerin' y'all a lead on they whereabouts."

The policeman did his best to stay cool on the other end, and answered, "Sir, we are utilizing every bit of CONCRETE evidence we have at our disposal. We have reason to believe they could have been kidnapped by associated criminals." The policeman carried on, "So, if you have any

CONCRETE information to divulge that may assist us in this case, then we will surely take it into consideration, Sir."

Roger took a moment to let that last statement sink in. He glanced over at Coach's smiling face as he sat in the rusted cart next to the decorated payphone. Ole Rog briefly contemplated the pros and cons of telling the police that Coach was found by the car that no longer existed. The old man knew it was the right thing to do, though and told this officer the truth.

"Well, I suppose I should inform y'all of the precious lil' boy I discover near the car two days ago." Roger reluctantly disclosed to the listener.

The officer snickered before answering, "Do you mean the car that only you allege ever existed, near your property?" his snicker turned into a chuckle after completing this question. As the officer continued, he added, "And Mrs. Morales was eight months pregnant, Sir. So, there is no way you could be in possession of her unborn child."

Roger was livid when he heard this response and took a few seconds to calm himself before reacting. "I am merely attemptin' to do the right thing. I know what I seen, and I know what I'm seein'. I can come on down to the station to show y'all what I am speakin' of."

The man on the other end was alarmed by this offer and promptly responded, "No. Sir, please do not do that. We are busy solving actual crimes and must utilize resources appropriately. Speaking of which, I need to get off the line here. So that we can free it up for impending distress calls. We know where you live. We will certainly reach out if we feel you could be of further assistance. Thank You."

Before Roger responded, the officer had hung up on him. "Son'bitch!" Roger said aloud, as he put the phone back on the hook.

Ole Rog had mused what to do next. "On one hand, the word has gotten around the station that Roger Brottle is a senile old man. So, to show up with a young toddler and a perceivably outlandish explanation on who the young lad is... Would almost certainly lead to the expulsion of Coach."

"Coach, they would stick ye butt right into the godforsaken system. Ye most certainly don' deserve such a future." Roger declared.

Roger had no idea how to raise a kid, or whatever Coach was, at the seasoned age of seventy-one. Ole Rog just knew what Coach had done for his sorrowful soul and knew that such a special being should not be wasted in such a bleak environment. "What is a man to do?" thought Roger. "I could go about searchin' for them Morales folk myself."

"What do ye think 'bout that, Coach?" Roger said towards Coach's juvenile and smiling face.

The duo hopped back into Ole Rog's truck with their gathered supplies and took the ride back to the old man's domain. The day was still relatively young, and they had plenty of daylight to work with for their initial search for Coach's parents. Roger whistled with content even though the situation was erratic. Coach smiled with glee even though he had no clue as to the calamity he was born out of. They were a remarkable couple, in an exceptional circumstance, looking for answers.

After returning home and unpacking the purchased items, the dynamic duo hit the forest in search of solutions but found themselves returned home, once again, in disappointment.

"I am sorry, Coach, I truly do wanna get ye back with ye loved ones," Roger admitted. But he quickly had a revelation, "Maybe Coach was home? Maybe I can be his loved one for now? At least until we find some answers." Roger finished his stream of hopeful thoughts before sharing a smile with Coach. The table was set with two bowls of vegetable slop.

The next day came about, Coach's young body subtly advanced again beyond any human scope of growth. Roger prepared their breakfast, plotted the area he wanted to search for the day, and gathered necessities for their journey. Roger was driven like he had not been for some time. It was important for him to at least try for Coach's sake. Coach could still not yet walk, but he was standing on his own now. Roger was astonished daily by the advancements of this living creature. He constructed a backpack in which he could slip Coach into during their explorations.

The two persisted with this routine for months: Vegetarian diets, searching for answers, the rapid development of Coach, and unsuccessful findings. Coach had outgrown his backpack and could now walk on his own. Roger had taught Coach basic life lessons and introduced Coach to literature. Coach would watch and read with a smile on his face. Always reassuring that even if he was not registering the information, he was pleasantly trying. It seemed like for every day that would pass, Coach would age several days physically. He was now almost three feet tall, walking around confidently and smiling always. Roger was elated to have Coach under his wing, even under the ambiguous conditions. He had always wanted a boy of his own, to teach and share life's experiences with. Roger knew this wonderful situation could not last forever. Eventually, Coach would need more than just Ole Rog and the solitude of the mountains.

"But how would society fare with such a special individual?" Roger pondered, on a nightly basis. He also understood that it was unjust to keep him from others, the planet will need Coach. He was never surer about anything else in his life. But until that bridge must be crossed, Roger would relish in every moment he had with Coach.

Chapter 6:

Roger and Coach had been together for well over a year now, searching the forest almost every day for traces of Denise and Jorge. They came up empty. Meanwhile, Coach quickly advanced. He now resembled a five-year-old adolescent boy. Roger often wondered what the cause was for such evolution, "Was it genetic? Disease? Supernatural?" he wondered until he realized that it was ultimately irrelevant. He loved Coach either way. Roger often sought after getting him tested to see if modern medicine could decipher the riddle, but he did not want Coach to become a science experiment. Thus, the two spent their days together in the great outdoors, and their nights together reading and smiling.

In the year 1999, Roger felt the need to search for Denise and Jorge fading from his conscience. He had made a trip back to the Morales's house in the prior year and found that the residence had been sold to another family. Ole Rog anonymously called into the police station to see where the Morales investigation had turned and found they had written the case off as an unsolved mystery. Ole Rog continued the search in the forest to keep both himself and Coach occupied, but it simply felt futile.

"Well, Coach, I don't think we will ever find ye parents. But they gone always be a part of ye." Roger reported to Coach on a crisp October afternoon. Unbeknownst of Coach's infantile consumption of his parents' turquoise remains.

It was Halloween morning when Roger felt a phenomenally gravitational pull towards town, where he unconsciously found himself next to Coach at a local saloon. The old man and the young boy sat at the dim bar together in perfect harmony while the television played the local news. A story of a horrific tragedy concerning a young couple with twin girls unfolded. Both these innocent girls died at five from a mutually shared, rare blood disease.

"Can ye please turn that on up, Sweetie?" Roger asked the bartender.

The story concluded through the television speakers: "This young couple lost both of their daughters, at the same time, and are too frightened to try to have kids again. Such a sad predicament for such a loving couple... "

Roger had heard all he needed to hear but was not sure how or when, he got to this old saloon. He finished the last salty sip of his warm beer and led Coach out of the door to their next destination. Roger was driving towards an undetermined location. Something was guiding them, and when he looked over at the adolescent marvel in his car, all he could see was a smile.

They drove around for thirty minutes through various neighborhoods, subconsciously turning this way and that until Roger slammed on the brakes. He was not sure what had come over him. Ole Rog immediately checked on Coach, only to consult that treasured grin. "Where are we?" reflected Roger.

"What are ye thinkin', Coach?" Roger asked his beloved companion.

Coach turned his pubescent head towards a small colonial house off to the right and pointed his short finger at the specified domicile.

"That's where we headin' then." Roger conceded to Coach's suggestion, and they exited from the truck.

As the two approached this house, Roger was struck by a feeling of inexplicable sadness he had not felt for the past year and a half with Coach. It was still early in this late Halloween morning, and there was a Fall chill in the stirring winds. They drew near the house steadily, and Roger let

Coach lead the way. Coach, led by some natural guide, hustled his way up the porch and knocked on the front door. To Roger's surprise, the couple they had just seen on the television answered the door to greet them both.

"Hello there, Young Man. How can we help you today? Trick-or-Treating does not start for some hours." The man spoke warmly and with a damaged smile.

"Aren't you precious, what's your name, Honey?" The woman at the door tenderly asked.

Coach met both of their sad eyes with his gracious smile. The woman cried, and ran back into the house, while the man stood in the entranceway with his eyes watering.

Roger caught up to the scene and introduced himself, and Coach, " Hey there, mister, my name is Roger, and this special fella here is Coach."

Tears had streamed down the man's cheeks before he could reply with an outstretched hand, "My name is Greg. I am so sorry about our appearance. We have had an incredibly woeful month." Greg attempted to wipe away the tears from his face before resuming, "What can I help you, fellas, with?"

"Well, I reckon we ought to step on inside and have a chat with y'all fine folk," Roger responded in a sincere tone.

Greg, being his generous and hospitable self, immediately waved them both inside the house.

"Let me just check on my wife, Paula. You guys make yourselves at home." Greg offered, as he was pacing away to console his distraught wife.

Roger stood in the foyer and turned to Coach, inquiring, "What's the plan here, Bud?!"

Ole Rog was partially confused and playing partially ignorant. Deep in his heart of hearts, he knew why Coach had led them here. He was just afraid of accepting the truth. The couple had returned together, in a frazzled state, to find Roger and Coach sitting silently on the couch in the living room.

"Hello Madam, my name is Roger." Ole Rog popped up from his seated position to greet the mourning mother. "We just seen y'all on the news earlier today. My deepest condolences for ye losses." He offered the grieving couple this sincere sentiment.

Paula felt the tears uncontrollably forming in her eyes again, she could barely speak, but moaned through a response, "Thank you, but what are you doing here exactly?" Greg turned his head towards Roger, out of genuine curiosity. The two looked engulfed in the blues.

"See that lil' fella smilin' over there on ye couch? That be Coach, and he a special boy." Roger informed them but could see confusion mounting in their eyes. "He lifted the sorrow from my ole soul over a year ago. He, or somethin', done guide me here to ye house."

The couple looked at each other to register this moment, and Greg eventually replied, "I am not sure what this all has to do with us. It has been a pleasure meeting you and your son, but we are grieving for our baby girls."

Roger put his arm gently on Greg's shoulder as to usher the couple towards Coach and said, "Just c'mon n sit with the youngin for a spell."

They both shuffled their weary feet over to the living room and sat down on the couch across from Coach. He was sitting there, smiling up at Greg and Paula, as they made themselves comfortable.

"Hello, Sweet Boy." Paula greeted Coach again, with a feeble smile and angst in her heart.

Coach stood up from the sofa and walked over to the couple. They were mesmerized by this little character, his calm but captivating manner and his beaming smile. Sweet Coach propped himself between the sorrowful couple and slipped his arms behind each of their backs. Directly after contact, Coach radiated a turquoise hue as the couple squeaked out clangs of astonishment.

Roger was watching from the far end of the couch, and tears rolled down from both eyes as he observed Coach's brilliance. He felt proud, proud of the fact that he had the pleasure of raising this special boy from his pupil stage. Proud that Coach was drawn back to civilization, so he could help others with broken hearts. Proud that he had remained fortified in his quest to find Coach's family and home. Ole Rog sat, weeping in awe, as he watched the misery lift from this kind couple's hearts.

Greg and Paula were now engrossed in the process and could feel a light peeking through their darkened spirits. They had felt a numbing that captured their whole bodies. The numbing transformed into a bright shiver that emitted intense rushes of reprieve from their sullen hearts. The intensity grew, the turquoise hue brightened, and the groans turned from misery to euphoria. An exorcism of despair was ousted from each Greg and Paula. They both leaned back on the couch as Coach kept his arms caressed around their backs. His shade of turquoise dimmed as the transaction seemed to come to its conclusion. Greg and Paula came to consciousness to jump from the couch and Coach's light embrace. Their faces were streaming tears that drenched their shirt collars, and they looked puzzled but rejuvenated.

Paula observed her living room filled with a strange old man sobbing and a young boy's turquoise glow fading from his skin. She bellowed, "What on Earth just happened?! That was unreal!"

The couple had been grieving their deceased twins for weeks now, and never thought they would ever recover any thread of the persons they once were. They both have intimately shared, with one another, their fears this incident would change their goodness. The optimistic spirit they both

worked so hard to maintain in their characters. Greg and Paula were
philanthropists and primarily functioned to share their light with others.
This recent and tragic event had blocked out their collective light. They
tried to support each other the best they could through the mourning process
but found it increasingly hard to recuperate.

Greg was startled to feel like 'himself' again and reflexively
shrieked, "Good lord!" out of pure, internal, serenity.

"What just happened?! How am I feeling so terrific suddenly?!"
Paula questioned anyone who cared to listen.

"I second that!" Greg agreed. The couple hugged one another with a
loving ferocity, holding their embrace for several seconds.

"I told ye, he a special boy." Roger chimed in from across the way.

Coach had reverted to his normal, olive-brown, skin tone, and his
eyelids weighed heavy under his youthful eyebrows. The youthful prodigy
had passed out after absorbing all the suffering he could from the couple.
All the adults in the living room smiled whilst studying this miracle of a
juvenile. He took away a lifetime of grief from three adults now, in his

relatively short existence on Earth. Each grownup wondered where this misery was transferred to. But they were already baffled enough trying to figure out what Coach was exactly.

Roger finally broke the silence by whispering, "Ye folk feelin' better now?"

Greg started in excitedly, "It was an unbelievable sensation, we were so overtaken by grief and after just five minutes here with your boy. I have felt unexplainable ease... I am not sure how to put it into words." Greg's enthusiasm made it hard for him to articulate.

Roger promptly interjected, explaining, "Please, Sir. I fully reckon what ye gettin' after. Like I say before, he done worked his magic on me as well. My Judy died over eight year ago now. When I stumbled upon this here youngin, I was merely countin' my days until I get to be with her 'gain. I found Coach in the forest near my property. Been lookin' for his parents for a year and a half now. I contact the police several time and not one of them care to listen to me."

Paula ecstatically interrupted, "You found him in the forest?!" her face wore expressions of shock and amazement. She was having a difficult time following this wild story Roger was telling, especially after being cleansed of such a cloud on her conscience.

Roger nonchalantly shook his head, yes, as to affirm Paula's question with normality. He proceeded with his story, "I found ole Coach in a valley by his parents' car, or what I reckon was his parents' car. He was naked 'n roamin' 'bout. When I came back with the police... The car was gone, and the damn forest had changed 'gain on me." Roger slapped his knee after making this ridiculous statement.

Greg now could no longer contain his questions, "When you say the forest changed again, what do you mean precisely?" He was consciously attempting not to sound condescending.

Roger swiftly replied, "The forest done evolved, or some damn aliens came in and cover up the scene. I don't know. I just can't call it. I got no good explanation for y'all. I am just tryna inform ye with the tiny bit of information I have myself." Roger glanced over at Coach as he repositioned himself on the couch. Coach was still sleeping off the exertion.

"So, how old is Coach?" Paula inquired. "He looks like he is five years old. But you said you found him a year and a half ago, as a crawling baby?!" Her curiosity was seeping from every pore.

Roger rehashed what had been described understanding how difficult this story must be to digest. But they did just experience something remarkable that has no definition. He could tell by the couple's tone they understood the circumstance. They were justifiably longing for any answers they could get. Amazed and overwhelmed, Greg and Paula were on the edge of their seats as they waited for Roger to continue.

"Coach and I went out a-searchin' for his ma 'n pa almost every day 'round the Smokies. He would grow like a human weed, every day a lil' longer, a lil' broader." Roger felt his eyes swell up as he described his only child's upbringing. "Such a good youngin, though. Never cry, never did whine. Just smilin' and noddin'."

Roger took a moment to gather himself before concluding his and Coach's tale "I am glad I decided to look after this here special boy and keep him outta harm's way. Coach taught me many lessons and I sought to return the favor. Somethin' on this day lead us here to y'all."

Greg and Paula sat in silence for one minute, absorbing this exotic material they were just bestowed. They passed their gaze between Coach and Roger, then unto one another briefly before Paula spoke up, "We will always remember our baby girls. But before Coach laid his hands on me, my heart was shattered into a million pieces. Now it is as full as the day those girls came into our lives."

Greg bowed his head up and down in accordance with what his wife had just disclosed. He looked at the sleeping boy while sympathetically asking Roger, "What can we do to repay you both? Anything to help, please just let us know." Greg met Roger's teary eyes with a passionate glare.

"Well ye see, I think that's just it. This boy need a proper home, one with two lovin' parents and community and all the things a delightful boy deserve... " Roger cleared his fickle throat to finish his train of thought, "... I would be honored if y'all two would accept this duty. I deem myself a good judge a character, and Coach was the one that done lead us here in the first place."

Roger freed his throat again to further his cause. But when he focused on Greg and Paula's faces, he saw them staring lovingly at Coach's resting frame. He knew he did not have to do any more convincing. Coach had found his new home.

Greg had his arm around his wife, and they both looked back at Roger, together. Paula took the lead by confirming, "We would love nothing more in this world than to continue raising Coach. It would be OUR honor, Roger."

Roger stood up to announce his departure, "Well, sun gone down soon... I best get to steppin'." He shifted anxiously towards the door to make his way out.

Greg stood up after him and placed his hand on Roger's shoulder to cease him momentarily, "Would you like to stay for supper at least, and wait to say goodbye to Coach?"

Roger replied earnestly, "It would only make this here transition more difficult, more for me than him. I am certain of it."

Ole Rog pressed his way out of this revitalized family's household. Roger took a moment to appraise his decision while studying Coach's new home from the exterior. He noticed the last name of the couple on their porch address label, 'Maker'. This reminded him he never told the Makers about the name on the registration, 'Morales'. Roger persisted towards his truck, thinking to himself, "Coach Maker sound pretty damn good to me." Ole Rog drove off with a smile and a new lease on life. He was satisfied with where Coach's mystic intuition brought them both.

Chapter 7:

Coach awoke from a well-deserved, multiple hour nap with a rumpled smile on his youthful face. His body was a bit longer still, and the young boy's bare feet a little wider. He searched the room for Roger's familiar grey beard and gentle eyes. Coach only found Greg and Paula quietly conversing on the adjacent couch. Coach felt nauseated from the agony he had absorbed through Greg and Paula, and he took several minutes to get his bearings.

"We never got candy for the children tonight, Greg!" Coach overheard Paula state to her husband. The two were cheerful, and enthusiastically dashing through their conversation. It was a beautiful sight to see for Coach, after what he recalled encountering when he and Roger first arrived.

Greg noticed that Coach was waking up from his slumber and said, "I am sorry, Buddy. Did we wake you?" he always had genuine concern in his voice.

Coach sat up straight on the couch and smiled at the duo. He then felt his eyes wandering, hoping to spot his comrade nearby.

Paula noticed the boy curiously searching, and clarified, "Roger is gone, Coach. He left you here with us. He wanted you to have a semi-normal life after all you have been through."

Coach shook his head, yes, as to concur with what Paula had just told him. However, he could not help the inflammation in his tear ducts. Some natural force was introducing a demonstration for the Maker couple. Coach let out a single, pale, turquoise tear that fell on the sofa seat. This tear immediately transformed into a small seedling that sprouted from the suede fabric. As two more tears departed Coach's moist eyes, they followed next to the first plantlet. Greg and Paula watched, astounded by what they were witnessing. Coach kept his head slightly cocked down and to the side, oblivious of the many sprouts forming around his pubescent legs. After the presentation finished, Coach peered up at Greg and Paula's spellbound expressions with an organic grin on his face.

"It's okay, Honey. You let it out, let the forest grow." Paula encouraged Coach with a consoling smile. Greg was speechless next to Paula. He was stuck staring with his mouth wide open.

After finally snapping back to reality, Greg unpredictably expressed, "You are a special boy."

Paula walked over to Coach and helped him off the couch. She noticed that some slits had formed on Coach's ill-fitted shorts. There must have been at least twelve sprouts developed on the couch. "Why had Roger never mentioned this phenomenon before? Had he never seen it?" Paula decided to just ponder on such thoughts, for now, she could save the discussion for later.

"How about we show you your new room, Coach?!" Paula asked the invulnerably smiley boy.

"It's right this way." Paula guided Coach down the hallway to the spare room across from their master bedroom.

"You know today is Halloween, Coach? Kids dress up in scary costumes and go around the neighborhood gathering candy. It sounds silly when I explain it like that, ha." Paula had laughed to herself after making the statement. Coach just intriguingly smiled at Paula as she explained occurrences he had never heard of and help him change into a new outfit. She grabbed some of Greg's older clothing that no longer fit him but was still far too large for Coach's juvenile body. A red shirt displaying 'Peace' and some blue athletic shorts would have to do for now.

Paula was elated whilst dressing her new 'son' and called out to Greg from the room, "Hey, Greg! How about you run to the store and get the kids some candy and Coach some suitable clothing?!"

"Sure, Hun," Greg responded with his patented sincerity. He investigated and plucked out the residual saplings Coach cried into their sofa.

The two boys embarked on the journey into the local shopping mall. Greg and Coach grabbed several bags of 'fun-sized' candies for the Halloween festivities. They stopped at a young man's clothing store to pick out a couple of sets of garb and then wandered around for a bit. Greg could see in Coach's bulging eyes he had never witnessed such a carnival of phenomena. All the lights, smells, colors, people, noises, it was all so exhilarating compared to his previously mountainous lifestyle. Coach held his smile to its full extent while they perused the food court.

The smell of cinnamon and sugar guided Coach to the pretzel stand where he stopped and stared at the booth. "Would you like one?" Greg insisted. Before he even waited for a response, Greg ordered one soft pretzel with all the fixings. The two silently sat at a table in the court and shared an enormous pretzel amongst the external swirls of sensations.

The boys packed back into the car with Coach still draped in Greg's old red and blue garments. The two headed back home to their mutually significant other. Paula had cooked dinner; tonight, they were having vegetable lasagna. Both Paula and Greg had taken on vegetarian lifestyles during their missionary travel days. One of the many lessons that philanthropy taught them along the route. This was an ideal transition for Coach. Ole Rog explained to Greg and Paula that Coach was raised on a strictly vegetarian diet for the time they had together.

The smell of garlic and onion wafted about the house as the boys entered the front door. "Coach!" Paula shouted from the kitchen. "Did you find something good to wear?!" she was an invigorated individual after the incredible events of this day's morning.

His smile was as bright as it had ever been, Coach felt the love returning into this house. Greg chimed in, "We got ourselves a pretzel. Right, Bud?"

Paula replied, concernedly, "I hope you boys did not spoil your appetites! Dinner should be ready in an hour or so." She returned to her project at hand, and Greg took Coach around his new home for a tour of the layout.

The threesome ate dinner together. They all shared titters while fulfilling their ravenous hungers. Most of the food had been finished, Greg and Paula commented on how they both have eaten little in months. Coach wore his proud smile while he adapted to his new surroundings. Greg filled up a deep salad bowl with sugary morsels for the ensuing Trick-Or-Treaters. The sun set, and the children commenced the roaming of the neighborhood. There were ghouls, ghosts, goblins, vampires, werewolves, witches, pirates, and all other styles of costumes mixing between properties along the streets.

The doorbell rang, "Treat-or-Treat!!" several children called from the porch. Greg opened the door to greet the youths and placate his role in this night's grandeur. Coach was standing behind Greg, smiling at all the interesting faces. He was already overwhelmed by the diversity he had encountered today. But Coach was enjoying every bit of it. The kids scampered off after they had gotten their treats. Coach ran after them, but Greg speedily caught up with the agile boy.

"Hold on there, Coach." Greg exclaimed as he scooped Coach up to bring him back in the house. He kept a smile on his face as Greg cradled him.

"Honey, I think I want to take Coach out for a little Tricks n' Treats." Greg announced while grinning down at Coach.

Paula agreed to hold down the fort while the two boys went around exploring on this Halloween night. They made cliché ghost costumes out of old sheets, simple and easy. The one Greg was using was not even white, but more of a beige. It did not matter; Greg loved Halloween and could tell

Coach was similarly fascinated. They set off from the porch, Greg held the

pillowcase they would use for accumulating treats in one hand and Coach's

hand in another. Greg could not see that prominent smile of Coach's but

could hear joyful gasps passing from the tiny ghost's fabric membrane.

Coach had not spoken a word yet, or possibly ever, for all the couple knew.

Thus, Greg handled calling the famous Halloween greeting for the two.

The night was cruising on by, hours had passed, children were

dispersing back to their homes, and porch lights were turning off. "But it is

only 9:15 pm!" thought Greg, as he checked his timepiece.

"We still got more in us. Right, Coach?" he rhetorically asked aloud.

The neighborhood quieted down while Greg and Coach wandered

along Harmony Street, three blocks over from the Maker's home. Greg was

racing to hit every possible home still participating in this dwindling

Halloween night. Along their hustled path, the boys walked past a dark,

dreary, and abandoned home at the end of the block. This home presided

over a large piece of land that the state owned but procrastinated in

renovating for the neighborhood's sake. Some foul act had happened on this

land, and the Earth felt poisoned. Coach was arrested by this harsh and deserted land. He stopped dead in his tracks and turned his ghostly head towards the property. After further examination, he saw the ground was covered with glass, trash, metal scraps, nails, natural refuse, and a bevy of other pollutants.

"What's wrong, Coach?!" Greg turned his head back and questioned. He found himself quite a few paces in front of Coach. Coach raised his finger to point at the forlorn estate to communicate some torment.

"It is quite the eyesore. Isn't it, Bud?" Greg stated as he walked back to where Coach had stopped. "We won't be walking up to that porch, Coach. Let's carry on, Buddy." Greg grabbed Coach's hand and led them through the rest of the block until all the porch lights had been dampened.

The boys returned home to an exciting welcome from Paula, "How was it, Coach, did you get lots of candies?!" Greg unsheathed the boy from his costume to reveal that charming smile. Coach's feet were bare again after discarding his new sneakers.

"I bet he's never had candy before," Greg said bluntly. "Let's crack a couple of these treats open. What do you say, Champ?"

The three sat around a pile of accrued candies. They laughed and sampled different flavors until they could no longer stomach any more sugar. Coach's smile was strong and stained with chocolate remnants. He had had his version of an extraordinary day. The couple could not participate in family or social events for the past year, due to the conditions of their perishing daughters. Greg and Paula thought about their daughters all day today, as they had every day prior, but they did not feel pain or sorrow. They focused only on the positive memories, the pleasant times they shared in such a short time frame together. It was a blessing. Paula woke up this Halloween morning with the same daunting worry she would never recover the internal light that facilitated her life. She worried that Greg would go down with her sinking ship. She worried. Then, this marvelous boy stepped through the front door and altered their futures in inconceivable ways. The bliss wound down as midnight approached, Coach was already passed out on the floor near the pile of candy. Greg lifted the sleeping boy, took him to his new room, and retired for the night with his wife.

Chapter 8:

The new day brought on a new month and with it, new growth. Paula was the first one up, and she checked in on Coach. He had fallen asleep in the red and blue outfit he wore all day, the one that seemed five sizes too big just yesterday. Today the clothes seemed to be only two to three sizes too large. It appeared as if Coach had grown half a foot overnight, now resembling an eight to ten-year-old. His feet had expanded, his neck and arms were longer, his hands wider. It was an abnormality, but this entire scenario was. Paula studied the bizarre growth of Coach for some time before she heard Greg's footsteps in the hallway.

"Hey Greggie, come check this out. Coach has grown quite a bit," she whispered to him in the hallway.

Greg walked through the entryway. He was yawning the morning away before concentrating in on the discernible expansion of this boy's body. "Holy hell, Paula!" he inadvertently blurted out.

Through all the commotion, Coach had roused from his slumber; he looked cloudy-eyed when he awoke. Coach noticed Greg and Paula standing in the doorway, which launched his daily smile.

"You want some breakfast, Bud?" Greg said with a shocked and alternating pitch in his raspy voice.

The three made their way to the kitchen area. Coach sat in the same chair as the previous night. This was to be his new-found seat at the table. Greg and Paula made waffles in the kitchen, coupled with an array of berries and miscellaneous fruits. As Paula poured syrup on Coach's waffles, his eyes lit up with great fascination. He had never sampled syrup, candy, or any of these sweet treats he had consumed in the last twenty-four hours. Coach hummed while he ate his breakfast, he had always loved music. That was one of the few bits of entertainment available while living in the mountains with Roger. Greg and Paula smiled at one another during the performance. Their hearts were full.

Greg and Paula discussed what the next course of action was for young Coach. "What age do you think he is anyway?" Paula challenged Greg with this inscrutable question.

Greg posed in his best deliberation face and said, "Well, he looks like he is nine today!" they both shared an innocent laugh at Coach's expense. The boy was still humming away as he finished his sticky plate.

"Let's just take the rest of the weekend and see if we can enroll Coach into one of the elementary grades sometime next week." Paula conceded.

"Sounds good to me. How about you, Coach?!" Greg asked over to the jubilant youngster.

Greg cleaned up the mess on the table as Paula took Coach to the bathroom to clean up the mess on him. She ran a bath for Coach to soak in and allowed them time to bond. As they did just that, Paula examined Coach's naked body. She noticed the development of his unique genitals; he did not look like a toddler in this region but more like a teenager.

"I suppose this is one way to gauge how old you are." Paula thought to herself as she helped Coach get settled in the tub. She wondered throughout the entire bath, captivated by this silently sweet, smiling boy.

Greg called into the bathroom from down the hall, "Hey, Hun. How about we take Coach to the park today? Show him around the neighborhood without a sheet over his face?"

"I think that sounds lovely!" Paula shouted back. She briefly speculated what neighbors might say or think, but quickly realized that people will always have their opinions. "But we have Coach," she whispered to Coach as he dried himself off.

Coach put on the largest set of clothing that Greg had purchased at the mall yesterday. It was snug but forgiving because of its elastic material. Coach finished dressing into his slightly ill-fitted tracksuit that provided warmth on this crisp November first. The Makers readied themselves, and made their way out of the house, feeling cheerful in their lives' status. Both Greg and Paula had their daughters on their minds but felt only exultation. The Makers all held hands while walking to the conveniently located city park. The sun was shining as they found the main trail that ran through the three-mile-long landscape.

The fresh air was brisk but sensational when combined with the heat of the day's glaring sun. Paula and Greg had been chatting with one another about Coach's future in the Maker family. They passed an impoverished and melancholy man on a park bench. Greg and Paula continued walking with their eyes faced forward, paying little regard to this downtrodden man.

Not that they did not care but more so because they were engulfed in the

conversation at hand. Coach, however, was immediately diverted to this

woeful bloke. He had freed himself from his new parents' distracted grasp

and strolled up to the horizontal man. The Maker adults were now ten feet

further up the path, and Coach was within arm's reach of this soiled

vagrant.

The man had a grimy beard, dirt-encrusted his pores across his

weathered face, and his clothing was coated with filthy markings. His eyes

popped opened as Coach straightened out his arm to contact the man's

shoulder. Greg and Paula, now 30 feet further along the path, stopped once

they realized Coach was not with them. In a panic, their heads bobbled

around in search of this elusive child. Once they turned around, in unison,

they spotted Coach with his hand on a resting homeless man. Confusion and

unease filled them both, and they sprinted back to their newly acquired

mystical boy.

Coach had begun to turn his rejuvenating, and turquoise, hue by the

time Greg and Paula sprinted. The homeless man's eyes rolled back, and his

body looked paralyzed. He squealed groans of sorrow and relief while

Coach's hue brightened. All Greg and Paula could do was observe in awe. They contemplated amongst themselves, "Is this what happened to us yesterday morning?" The grumbles from the man grew louder, and Coach's turquoise sharper. It was as if the shade of color indicated the degree of pain Coach was releasing. This man had elevated levels. The process carried on for a full minute before the turquoise tone faded from Coach's skin. The homeless man popped up from his previously horizontal position and whimpered with a reverent smirk on his face.

"Thank ye, Child! I'm not sure what ye are, but I reckon ye one divine being." The man exclaimed and rushed off the bench towards some unspecified objective. Perhaps he would spread his fervor with others or make amends for past wrongdoings, only time would tell.

A young Coach was capsized over the same bench the man just bolted from. He could not fight the struggle to remain conscious. His new parents, having witnessed the entire phenomenon, helpfully hurried over to the cataleptic Coach. Greg lifted the fatigued boy and propped Coach's drowsy body over his shoulder.

"Let's go home," Paula concernedly voiced. The ruffled family rerouted back to their abode.

Coach slept the day away after relinquishing another stranger of his grief. Paula and Greg caucused for the rest of the day, rehashing what they observed. The Maker couple discussed future options for Coach and vented their worries to one another. As the day slipped away, Greg and Paula realized they had not eaten since the morning. The Maker pair swiftly rustled up some grub, checked on the depleted Coach, and then retired their tiresome minds for the night.

Chapter 9:

It was 3:17 am when Coach stealthily, and intuitively, made his way out of his new home. A gravitational force was guiding his enchanted body to an unidentified site. The night was dark and full of silence. Coach stammered around the block, wearing only his tight underwear and a skin-tight tee-shirt. Coach was being pulled somewhere, and he had no control over where. His feet were bare, and his breath was visible in front of him. Only, Coach's eyes were not open. Most folks would call this sleepwalking, but his direction and pace signified this was something unique; this was

Coach-walking. Eight minutes of vigorously chilly night strolling led Coach to that abandoned corner lot on Harmony Street. The one that Coach was halted by the previous night. The one that looked like it was used for something terrible and that was strewn with polluted Earth.

Coach finally made it past the property fencing and onto the polluted land. His feet felt fiery for the first time during this barefoot walk. As soon as his skin touched this tarnished ground, he felt queasy. His body lightly quaked in protest of what it was in contact with. Coach's primal senses were stirring about, and his body conformed to an unorthodox, hunched position. A few seconds passed before Coach felt a violent rush erecting from deep in his loins. The boy braced himself as a surge of turquoise bile came spewing from his adolescent mouth. His trajectory was extensive, and the radius in which he covered was vast across this wasteland. The substance covering the ground was mostly fluid. However, the fluid contained tiny spores which promptly rooted through the turquoise sludge that now enveloped the front half of the property.

This magical brew that exited Coach was rapidly propagating and flourishing across most of this parcel. Trees were progressing through their lengthy lifecycles in a matter of minutes, and vines were immediately spreading across the decaying wood structure of the evacuated house. Thick patches of wild bushes were densely bursting through the trash-laden surface, and tall patches of ferns interloped between the newly developed foliage. It was a marvelous sight to behold. Yet, no one was there to see it. As Coach finished unleashing the turquoise mixture from his gullet, he quickly collapsed on the soft and redefined sector of earth.

Meanwhile, back at the Maker house. Greg had awoken during the early morning around 4:20 am to relieve his bladder. In his journey to the commode, he stopped to peek after Coach. To his absolute shock, he found the bed empty and Coach nowhere to be found. Greg contemplated waking up Paula but then saw the front door ajar as he peered down the hallway. Impulsively, Greg grabbed his coat from the hook on the wall and rushed through the doorway. He figured that he could search for Coach before assuming the worst had happened. "Hell, maybe it was Roger." Greg struck a chord in his brain while wandering the neighborhood. Greg was now approaching a jogger's pace in pursuance of his peculiar, and missing, new son.

"Coach!?" Greg called out as he continued jogging down the road. He had made several laps around nearing blocks before refining his methods.

"He has only seen a small section of the neighborhood. Maybe he stuck to the ground we covered on Halloween?!" Greg projected to himself. He racked his brain to remember every detail about that night.

Greg fretted potentially tragic outcomes coursing through his psyche. He commenced on the route, screaming, "Coach!" along the way. As Greg approached the end of Harmony Street, he was astonished by the breathtaking panorama. What was once a repulsive stretch of acreage was now a miraculously stunning estate filled with sumptuous greenery, Greg was entranced. He was standing in the road, perplexed by this inexplicable imagery. Abruptly, Greg connected the dots, remembering what they witnessed form out of Coach's tears. Mr. Maker jolted towards this environmental utopia after convincing himself that Coach had something to do with it. To his accord, he found the young man lying on a silky patch of elevated moss perfectly sustaining Coach's comatose physique.

Greg carried Coach back to their home for the third time in two days. He was still in awe at what Coach had done to that property but merely gratified to have found the boy. It was now past five in the morning. Greg inconsiderably slammed the door upon his return home. He was far too puzzled and alarmed to practice courtesy at this moment and woke Paula up with the crashing of the door. As she rubbed the morning from her eyes, Paula zoned in on Greg, holding a motionless Coach on the sofa.

Paula scurried over to the two, fell to her knees to put her hands on Coach's head, and squealed, "What is the meaning of this?!" she bawled hysterically, glaring up at Greg, awaiting answers.

Greg did not know how to formulate an explanation but did his utmost to describe what he stumbled upon just an hour ago.

"Should we take him to the hospital?" Greg sputtered as he trembled from the overwhelming fluctuations of emotions. They both checked Coach's pulse frequently to reassure themselves that he was still alive, he was.

Paula revisited their past year of long hospital outings, experiments, inconclusive results, and their general discouragement in modern medicine.

It had been a year of medical disappointments and an objective curiosity for testing on their daughters' rare blood disease. Greg and Paula barely got to see their children in those last three months. The girls were quarantined where the doctors had permission to apply any clinical trials they thought might help. The doctors filled their appetites for discovering innovative cures. Congruently, two living beings dwindled at an accelerated rate with each administered trial. All Paula and Greg could do was watch helplessly and listen to each passing doctor express, "We are doing everything we can." The whole experience was grueling. It did not foster a trusting bond between them and the medical industry. After Greg was quietly transported back to those confronts, he agreed that industrialized science would take this supernatural boy from them to gather 'data'.

"What should we do then?!" Greg asked, eagerly longing for any sensible answer that could help in this quandary.

"We do what we have always done, love and support," Paula confidently responded.

They placed the boy back into his bed so he could continue recovering. It was as if he had amassed his full capacity of sorrow from various individuals. Nature, or some transcendent guide, had led Coach to that human-contaminated land. Here he could discharge the transformed, and absorbed, sorrow to return it unto the Earth from which it ultimately came. Constructively, it seems, Coach possesses the paranormal ability to convert this anguish into something productive and beautiful.

Greg placed Coach down on the bed and turned around towards Paula with amazement still seized across his face. "Paula, you have to come to see where I found him... What he did. How he did, what he did... " Greg stuttered and jumbled his words around. He was still shocked. It had been an unrivaled two-days of life.

"I'm not sure we should leave Coach alone," Paula worriedly stated.

Greg reassured her that Coach would be fine, and they would not take long; he could hardly contain himself any longer. The couple left the house to make their way over to Harmony Street, where the alchemy happened. Upon approaching the formerly desolate corner lot, they saw the perimeter saturated with neighbors, curious civilians, news crews, and police cars. Every person had their eyes propped open-wide in bewilderment at the irresistibly gorgeous plant life plugging this area. Paula walked up to the scene slowly, making sure not to rouse any suspicious

individuals, but Greg promised there was not a soul outside this early

morning. At least that's what he recalled in his flabbergasted state.

"It is the most beautiful thing I ever did see!" they overheard Mrs.

Prelim say, Greg and Paula's neighbor of eight years.

"We were sick of lookin' at that goddamn dump! This is much

better!" another neighbor yelled out.

The Maker's gingerly moved through the crowd. They were

listening to the prodigiously positive comments about this magnificent piece

of earthly beauty. Paula observed every inch of the terrain with great

admiration. She had always been a lover of gardening, horticulture, and an

advocate for the Earth-friendly practices of life. Paula could not take her

sights off this renovated land, except to meet Greg's eyes for a

complimentary gawk. They both now occupied proud grins on their faces as

to display their gratification for their special lad. The Makers only wished

they could make the announcement. That they are fostering a special child

with innately restorative characteristics... But they also knew that would

spur a frenzy on Coach's dear head.

"Shit, Coach!" Paula bellowed towards Greg. They had been gone for almost an hour, stewing in the fruits of Coach's labors.

The Makers slipped away from the buzzing crowd to make their way back home. Once they arrived, they both made the journey to Coach's room. He was still stationary and conked out from the radical exertion. Greg and Paula rejoiced in the living room for the remainder of the day. They discussed how Coach could have created that garden, how he absorbed their sorrow and the homeless man at the park. What Ole Rog had told them about Coach and everything they had witnessed until now. It was a horde of speculations mixed with observations and everything between. Greg and Paula reviewed their mutually gathered materials for well over three hours.

"So, do you think Coach is some sort of angel?" Greg inquired, mulling over any suitable answers they could cling to.

"For all we know about him, perhaps!" Paula corroborated; she could not plausibly eliminate that as a possibility.

There was a rustling in Coach's room. He was waking up from his slumber. As Coach walked down the hallway to greet his guardians, he felt a pressure around his neck and chest. Coach had outgrown the clothing he had on. He tore through the underwear. His shirt was still tautly stretched across his broadened chest, and the rigged collar was subtly cutting off circulation through his neck. Coach trudged his way to the living room and smiled as his new parents made ghastly noises back at him.

"Coach, are you okay!?" Greg asked as the two swiftly soared to Coach's aide.

Coach returned a pleasant smile as he was laboring to breathe, his face turned a light blue. Paula ran to the kitchen to grab a pair of scissors.

"Careful now, Coach," Paula advised as she cut away the collar from Coach's enlarged neck.

Coach gasped for air, never surrendering his smile. Greg and Paula helped him disrobe from the remaining rags he had sagging from his further evolved frame. Greg went to his closet to pull out more of his older clothes. This time, he was confident in the fit. Greg's clothes were now only one size too large on Coach. The Maker's had witnessed a toddler explode through his adolescence within three days.

Paula replayed these episodes in her head. She was formulating the sequence of time from when Coach performed his voodoo, to his immediate inertia, and then to his subsequent physical expansion. It made sense to her exotically and mystically, at least the pattern did.

Paula could no longer suppress her theory, probing, "What if these 'turquoise' encounters are causing Coach to age rapidly?" neither of them could confirm or deny.

"As Roger told us, Coach did the same turquoise expulsion to him as well. Him, you, me, the man in the park. Who knows who else?!" Paula dialed in her train of thought, as she and Greg were in the kitchen preparing a salad for dinner.

Paula was on a roll now, she continued with her conjecture, "What if Coach can only contain so much absorbed agony before he has to expel it from his body?!" she felt the excitement one gets when he or she is on the verge of completing a puzzle.

"So, you are insinuating that the eruption of vegetation over on Harmony is the byproduct of Coach's gift?" Greg questioned, deriving his destination as to where Paula's train was heading.

"Perhaps?" Paula sharply replied and shrugged her shoulders before setting the table for dinner.

Coach was seated at the table, smiling, his feet able to touch the ground now. He had pubescent and gentle hair forming on his upper lip, though his smile was still unadulterated. The Maker family sat around the table, crunching through their dinners, and recollecting the day's events. There was no need to further expand on their perceived theories, not tonight. Paula and Greg knew that Coach is on this Earth to spread goodness and relinquish angst. Whatever else is in store for Coach has yet to be unveiled. And until he is confronted with the next predicament, Greg and Paula will do their utmost to pay back the love that Coach has delivered.

Chapter 10:

The next day began with a mutual sigh of relief between Greg and Paula. They were comforted by Coach's body having not grown since they had dinner last night. Feasibly, Coach could have grown in a minute and ordinary, style, but that would be typical for humans. It was the first Sunday of November, and Greg popped on the morning news. The top story of today consisted of the revamped corner lot on Harmony. The one that

Coach had transmuted early yesterday morning.

"Look what you did, Coach! You brought about a spectacle. People

are crazed after what you exhibited." Greg declared while turning the

volume up...

The news reporter stated, "... There are now reports that a homeless

man was squatting inside the decaying walls of this ruined house, on this

discarded property. He is reported to be dead. Strangled by the spate of

encroaching vines and foliage that appeared during the night, just last night.

Unfortunately, calamity has to put a damper on this divine phenomenon... "

Greg quickly turned the TV off as he heard his wife approaching the

living room. When he glanced over at Coach, he saw the same smile he had

fallen in love with. Although maybe it was different. Greg knew Coach

could understand English. He knew Coach had understood what the news

reporter just said. "But maybe Coach was unaware of what he had done,

what he was capable of doing. Did he recall anything that had happened

yesterday, or was he fully aware of his actions?" Greg's mind raced through a plethora of questions and concerns about the matter, and about the individual, they had just taken in.

"Who is hungry?!" Paula spouted as she finished her trek down the hallway.

Both Greg and Coach had gotten up and transitioned over to the dining room table without answering the question.

"I suppose actions speak louder than words." Paula laughingly announced as she made her way to the kitchen to make mushroom omelets for the boys.

Greg nervously fidgeted with his fingers as his hands were clasped. He glanced over at Coach and saw a smile he could no longer categorize. Doubt had charged into Greg's mind, and he knew that he might never get the truth. For some odd reason, this discontentment made Greg's skin crawl. He believed that after all he had witnessed, there was no way Coach had maliciousness in his soul. Yet, he had only known this being for less than three days now. Paula was whistling to herself in the kitchen as she plated the first, piping hot, omelet, and brought it to the table. She served Coach first, and he was famished. Greg watched the kid inhale the omelet with a sour look on his face.

Paula came back in with the second plate, and Greg unexpectedly revealed, "I forgot I left something important at the office." The man stood up and departed from the house without another word. Both Coach and Paula looked at the closed door in sheer bafflement before continuing about their morning together.

Greg was having himself a panic attack against the front of the garage as he achingly leaned on the aluminum door, across from his vehicle. He plopped himself in the driver's seat after the attack subsided. There he sat and reflected on the news that had just emerged from the scene on Harmony Street. Mr. Maker was compelled to roll past the scene to see for himself. Greg was always one that cherished life, no matter what the circumstances or form. That's why he had been more shattered by the death of his innocent daughters than he ever cared to burden Paula with. Hence, he simply could not abide by murder, whether it was accidental or otherwise.

After several minutes, Greg started the car and reversed out of the driveway. He transiently found himself back at the house on Harmony Street. Greg parked his car around the block and walked his way to the active scene on the property, where there were two cop cars stationed.

Without hesitation, Greg confronted the first cop he came across, "Hello there, Officer. How are you today?"

The cop turned and replied, "I am doing well, Sir. What can I assist you with?"

"Just curious about what's going on here, I live three blocks over." Greg provided context for the stiff officer.

He hesitated before responding, scanning the area for any lingering patrolmen, "Sir, it is one of the wilder situations I have seen on duty... " His voice lowered in case anyone was listening, "... We found a man in the house. It was reported on the news today, but now the man is gone."

"Gone!? What on Earth do you mean?" Greg exclaimed with honest and vested, curiosity.

The policeman shook his head to sympathize with Greg's confused tone of voice, "We saw the man yesterday when we discovered this wild scene. He was wrapped up in vines and roots. Total mess... Today, he is gone."

"But you're sure there was a man in there?" Greg reiterated.

"Certain," the officer affirmed. "Maybe the plants ate him. You know, like decomposed his body for fertilizer." The cop added to end his stint in the conversation.

Greg turned around and cringed. He walked right past his car. He sauntered past his house; he strode. He needed the time to clear his head, to make sense of this. "If the body is gone, then maybe the memory could be too." Greg served out rationales in his cranium. He realized that the good Coach has bequeathed upon their lives far outweighs this accidental incident. Mr. Maker won the argument with Greg, once again, and he felt comfortable enough returning home. The car ride home was better than the initial departure.

"This Coach found us for a reason. He is more than just a boy. Remember that." Greg openly repeated this as his mantra during the short ride. When he pulled up in the driveway, he had himself convinced.

"Where the hell did you run off to, Greg?!" Paula accosted Greg when he plunged through the front door.

"I-I-I had my other credit card at the office. I thought we might need it with a new member of the family." Greg lied to his wife, something he rarely did. He could not bear to tell her the honest answer.

She looked over at him skeptically, replying, "You had to go get it today?! Right while we were about to have breakfast. While we are still on a bereavement period?!"

Greg works for a nonprofit organization specializing in building educational infrastructures in third-world countries. He was not due back at the office for another week.

Greg mustered up the internal audacity to lie again to his wife, and told her, "I am unnerved, Paula. I am just besieged by questions and concerns about the past couple of days. Reservations about the young boy, or man, we just accepted in our lives." This felt more believable than the initial response, and it was.

"I am too, Greggie. It has been quite the chaotic two-day spree." She comfortingly agreed with Greg's sentiment. The pair embraced. Greg had his chin on Paula's head as they held their hug. Greg could see Coach smiling in his direction, chills ran down his spine.

For the rest of the week, the Maker family progressed with their daily routines. Paula would provide Coach with materials for reading and she tested his competency in writing. Greg finished projects around the house he had delayed for the past year. He called Coach in on most, so he could demonstrate for the young man. Greg's unease around Coach receded throughout the week. Greg and Paula took the week's end to contact the local elementary school. Paula felt that Coach's reading and writing competency were both well into the high school percentile, but his stature was that of a fifth or sixth-grader. Coach had yet to speak a word around either of them. So, they both deemed him mute. It would be easier for everyone this way.

"Do you think we should be putting Coach right into school?" Paula solicited Greg, after they had discussed this situation for days.

"It will be good for all of us. I work all day. You participate in several charities and assist me with my responsibilities. It'll be good for him to sociali-, be around other kids that are of the same ag-, kids that look like him!" Greg emphatically finished the response.

Paula had decreased her workload tremendously to become a stay-at-home mom for their daughters. She had gotten comfortable with this lifestyle but always informed Greg of her desire to connect with the vast groups of less fortunate people in the world. Paula was a true empath, born to help others, and she recognized this as the main proponent of her identity. Getting into some altruistic activities made her tremble with anticipation. But she was still willing to continue said lifestyle for Coach.

"I suppose I would be open to getting back up on that horse!" Paula finally coincided with Greg's notion.

The Maker parents placed Coach into sixth grade at the local elementary school. Paula opted to get involved in two of her previous charities, Greg resumed back at work on Monday. The family, or Greg and Paula, had determined they would continue advancing as individuals.

"Good luck, everyone." Greg pronounced, on that Monday morning, just before he departed for work.

They all had similar times scheduled, in early November, to commence and recommence their enlightening journeys. Coach was escorted by faculty officials to the inside of the elementary school. He took fifteen minutes to get acclimated to the lights and aromas wafting through the exposed corridors. A class instructor chaperoned Coach while he swiveled his head back and forth. Coach was surveying, from room to room, as he made it down the hallway to the cafeteria. During this foreign excursion through the school, Coach's smile greeted multiple individuals and most shared a grin back. Except for one boy, Jerry Dingle. Jerry was infamously known as the school's bully. Coach's smile remained fortified when he encountered Jerry's troubled scowl through a classroom window.

Paula had agreed to let them familiarize Coach to the academic setting for only two hours on day one. She adamantly explained to the adults that Coach was a special boy. Paula attempted her best to articulate how special of a boy Coach was before he started his first day. But she received mundane reactions from the underwhelmed teachers and faculty members, who commonly hear from most parents about how special their children are. The day conducted harmlessly, and Paula came to pick Coach up after his two-hour tour. Just before his mother arrived, Coach noticed a man exuding despair from his human apertures. This man was the faculty custodian. He was drearily hunched over as he plodded through his sanitary duties. Subconsciously, Coach left the grip of the chaperon and made a course directly over to Frank, the janitor. Before he made it to the man, he was regripped by the chaperon, and brought back to the lobby of the school where his mother was waiting.

"Coach! My sweet Coach, how was your first day of school!?" Paula asked animatedly, believing that Coach's perpetual smile would transform into words one of these days.

Paula redirected her attention to the chaperon and principal standing next to her, reiterating, "I know I explained that Coach is mute, but he also has an eccentric intuition. Something that I ask you all to, please, be aware of during his time here."

Mrs. Maker grabbed Coach's expanded palm, and the two left the school for the day. "How's about we get some ice cream!?" Paula offered to Coach as they approached her car.

The two sat in the ice cream parlor and methodically relished in the satisfaction of their frozen treats. It was getting towards evening time now, and Greg was due home any minute. So, Paula initiated the cooking of dinner. They all sat together as a family and reviewed the day's events. Each member of the family had their own stories to tell, but Coach only spoke through his smiling face.

"How do you think he did today?" Greg asked Paula as they cleaned the kitchen table and wound down for the night.

"All that precious boy does is smile. If that is any indication, then I think it went well." Paula stated, hoping that she was right.

Chapter 11:

The next day launched Coach's first full day of school. Paula walked him to the lobby, where Ms. Plankton was there to greet him. Ms.

Plankton was a gentle woman that loved her job, she had a profound passion for educating the developing minds of kids.

"Hello there, Sweetie. I am Ms. Plankton, and I'm gonna be your teacher this year." She warmly embraced Coach, and concentrated on their visual connections, knowing he could not verbalize.

Coach let Ms. Plankton guide him to the classroom, where she introduced him to all the students. All the kids were receptive to the newcomer's arrival, except for Jerry. Jerry had been held back a grade for a learning disorder, and he came from an abusive family. Most days, Jerry could contain his anger around the rest of the bunch, but something about a cheerful face enraged Jerry beyond belief. Coach had the cheeriest face in the entire class. He was beaming in front of the others. It was exciting for Coach to be around so much youth. He loved to read, learn, and listen.

Coach did not feel fearful. Only in severe situations did it ever surface in the young man. Coach has felt no emotions that most humans contend with. He was a human born of unusual circumstances. Thus, he portrays extraordinary characteristics. Coach is selfless by nature. His inconsistently aging body meant nothing to him. His motives are piloted by some supernatural source. Coach exists to alter people's lives for the better.

He is not driven by social status and esteem like many of these youngsters

are. Coach's reason for being created in the cruel manner he was, has yet to

be revealed. Or perhaps, he was purely cultivated by these extenuating

conditions to relieve the sorrow of man while he roams the Earth. Coach

does not know. Paula and Greg do not know. Roger did not know. Only a

celestial being may know the truth. Only time will unravel this ball of

divine twine.

After Coach had been ushered to his assigned seat, Ms. Plankton

initiated today's lesson with mathematics. Coach kept his face down in his

textbook, absorbing all the fresh content they offered. Hours passed,

children exchanged opinions amongst one another, and the lessons

continued until the lunch bell rang. As the kids all arose at the stifling

clatter of the bell, Coach followed suit. Young Coach found himself at the

back of the funneling herd, where Jerry was awaiting him.

"What's up, Newbie?!" Jerry sneeringly questioned Coach. Jerry

was a similar size to Coach, but thicker in almost every area. Coach had a

lean build, pliable looking as if the world had stretched him out prematurely, which it had. All Coach could do is reply to Jerry with a sincere smile.

"The fuck ye smilin' at, Dumb Shit." Jerry instantly grew frustrated by Coach's adjoining presence. He reached out and lightly shoved Coach against the concrete wall in the hallway. Laughing hysterically, Jerry was enjoying his superficial dominance. As the delayed Ms. Plankton followed the class, she saw Jerry scattering from an assaulted Coach.

"Jerry! You get back here this instant!" Ms. P hollered after Jerry, but he had passed through the cafeteria doors.

"I am so sorry about that, Coach." Ms. Plankton consoled Coach as she helped him gather his balance. "That boy is troubled. He has a bad situation at home. His parents are neglectful and abusive. Try your best to avoid him. I will certainly help where I can." Ms. P explained the scenario as she marched with Coach to the cafeteria.

Once they strolled through the cafeteria doors, Coach was immersed in a cornucopia of boisterous sounds and curious smells. Children were laughing, screaming, consuming, and dashing around the communal tables. It was absolute pandemonium, but Coach's smile arched deeper as he took in the parade of vibrations. Ms. P assisted Coach through the lunch process.

She showed him where to get his food and elaborated that he could pick any

table he would like to sit at. Coach followed the instructions, pointed at all

the vegetarian options available, and the lunch lady served him his cuisine.

When he picked an empty spot to sit, he was greeted by the other children

who did not comprehend the mute disability. They continued asking Coach

questions, and he would merely retort with his patented smile.

While lunch dwindled and most kids escaped outside, or back to

class, Coach found himself in a nearly empty cafeteria. Frank, the

custodian, meandered into the lunchroom to clean up after the children had

finished. This man exuded great misery. Coach was immediately drawn to

his sad aura. Coach stood up from his bench-seat at the rectangular table

and made a beeline for an unsuspecting Frank. Before Frank even had a

chance to introduce himself, he felt the tingling sensation of agony retiring

from his heart. He was stuck in a paralyzed state against one of the emptied

tables. Frank thought he noticed a turquoise glare out of his peripheral view

before his eyes rolled back into his skull. One minute passed, and Frank was

released from this strange, encapsulating hold. He quickly turned around to see a turquoise fared kid passed out on the floor. The hunch in his back had straightened, his shoulders were lighter, and his soul felt brighter. Frank was happy and confused all at once.

Frank reached down to scoop up the unconscious boy, noticing the turquoise shade fading from his skin. He blurted, "What the hell are you, Kid?" He felt great like he had not felt in some time. Frank rushed from the cafeteria, with Coach in his arms, unknowingly leaving behind an involuntary spectator.

The custodian rammed his extended leg through the school's medical office door, shouting, "Someone come quick! This kid needs some attention!"

The school nurse dropped her nail filer and instructed Frank on where to place Coach, "Put him down on that table. What's wrong with him, what happened?" The nurse fired off a round of questions.

Frank tried his best to respond, "I-I-I am not quite sure, honestly. This boy laid his hands on me, turned turquoise, and passed out. I have never felt better in my life!" He was struggling to translate through his unstable spate of reactions.

Immediately, Frank realized how ridiculous his answer must have sounded and retracted his previous statement, claiming, "I honestly have no goddamn clue."

The nurse conducted the fundamental tests on Coach's inactive body. She tested his heart rate, blood pressure, and examined his pupils.

"Everything seems to be in order, isn't this the new kid? Maybe he has a flair for the dramatic." The nurse announced as she callously rescinded back to her nail filing.

Frank gave a disgruntled look towards the nurse and left to retrieve someone more compassionate. He ran across Ms. Plankton in the hallway and uncovered what had just transpired. Ms. P insisted Frank lead her to the fatigued child, at once.

When they arrived in the infirmary, Coach was as still as he had been. Ms. P, Frank, and the nurse discussed the series of events that occurred. It had grown into the afternoon and Ms. Plankton got her story straight before she called Paula Maker to explain what happened. Frank offered to keep watch over the boy while the nurse had her lunch, and Ms. P made the call to Coach's mother. Frank was a rejuvenated man, but he did not know how to articulate his sudden transformation. So, he offered to do his part in making sure this Coach stays breathing.

The phone rang two times before Paula answered. Ms. Plankton sighed before divulging the stories of today, "Hello, Mrs. Maker! This is Patricia Plankton, Coach's new teacher. I am sorry to have to inform you of some deviations from a smooth first day for Coach." She attempted to ease into the explanation.

"Did he pass out?" Paula said, almost casually. "I told you he is a special boy."

"That he is, Mrs. Maker. Frank, our trusted custodian, asserts to us that he had an encounter with Coach. And then he passed out, yes... But we had our school's nurse check all his vitals, and he is doing fine. Just resting." Patricia steadily portrayed the facts.

"Would you like us to call an ambulance?" Ms. P persisted.

Paula's voice heightened momentarily, "No! That will not be necessary. I will leave to come to pick him up directly." She hung up the phone and primed herself to retrieve Coach.

Ms. Plankton returned to the infirmary with a quizzical expression on her face. She was not expecting the responses she received from Mrs. Maker. Patricia was certain that Paula's voice would have been borderline hysterical. It was quite the opposite, she answered in a relaxed tone. Ms. P informed Frank that Coach's mother was on her way to retrieve the boy. Ms. Plankton had to return to her classroom to resume the children's lessons for the day.

"His name is Coach, eh?" Frank acknowledged and chuckled to himself, "quite fitting."

Paula rushed through the school's entrance, and briskly jogged her way around the faculty until she passed the medical center.

"Coach!" she called as she opened the door and spotted her special lad lying on the examination table.

Frank, now having rectified his stature, presented his palms in a halting motion towards Paula as she came charging in the room. "Ma'am, he is doing fine. He is just exhausted, and I think I know what from. Can I carry him to your car for you?" Frank offered so that the two could chat privately.

"That would be very helpful, thank you." Paula accepted Frank's offer. She could see the clarity in his eyes, she knew he was the one Coach exorcised.

Frank gently nestled his arms under Coach's neck and knees, with his six foot-four-inch frame and bulky physique, he made the lift look easy. The colossal custodian carried Coach through the school hallways and out the main entrance with Mrs. Maker.

Frank politely asked, "I do not mean to offend, but what is he?" looking down at Coach's dormant body as he was referring to him.

"No offense taken. He worked his same magic on us about two weeks ago. We were gifted this specimen by another who had experienced his abilities as well." Paula retorted to Frank's question.

"My wife and son were murdered two years ago. I was just reaching the point where I had fully suppressed my harmful emotions... But they were never really banished. Not until this boy, here, rid them from my spirit." Frank subtly elevated Coach in his arms while referencing the respite.

Paula smiled at the man's admiring stare he gave Coach and recognized that she could be candid with him, "Coach will most likely look different tomorrow. Most likely larger, more mature. This seems to be the pattern after he 'exorcises' someone," she comfortably explained.

"Don't worry about a thing, Mrs. Maker. I will keep my eye on this guy... " Frank assured Paula as he loaded Coach's carcass in the back of the car. "... And don't worry about that irritable Jerry Dingle, either. I will make sure he does not pick on Coach anymore. Not while I am around." Frank reassured her further.

"Someone was picking on Coach today?!" Paula bitterly countered. She was more so curious than angry.

"Yeah, Ms. Plankton told me that sad little shit had a run in with Coach. His parents are horrible people, cruel and irresponsible. They have left Jerry here for several hours after the school day's finished. He has shown up to class with bruises on his arms, face, legs; you name it." Frank elaborated while shaking his head, from side to side, in general distaste for people like that.

"Ah, I see. That is truly unfortunate. Did this Jerry seem any different after his confrontation with Coach?" Paula quizzed Frank as she entered the driver's seat.

"Not to my knowledge, Ma'am. He seemed like the same furious little shit when I saw him in the lunchroom." Frank concluded his dialogue in the conversation before shutting the driver's door.

"Thank you, Frank. Please DO keep an eye on our Coach... And call me Paula." She ended the conversation with a smile and headed home with Coach secured in the back seat.

On the ride home, Paula envisioned Coach's exorcising of Frank in the cafeteria. She also visualized Jerry's altercation with Coach before lunch. "It sounded like Jerry put his hands on Coach. And it sounded like Jerry is one sad young boy. How did Coach avoid relinquishing Jerry of his pain and suffering?" Paula pondered on these discrepancies in her understanding of Coach. She adoringly checked on Coach in the rear-view mirror. The two made it home, and to Paula's surprise, Greg was in the driveway waiting for their arrival. Paula had called Greg at work just before she left for the school to update him on the situation. She did not expect him to dash home, though.

"What are you doing home, Greg?!" Paula exclaimed.

"Who else is going to lift this young man out of the car?" Greg countered with a smirk on his face. He was right though, Coach now had the lean body of a teenager and weighed nearly 100 pounds. Paula might have been able to strenuously drag the poor kid inside.

Once they all congregated indoors, Paula gave Greg the entire rundown of today's events. Greg had all the same questions as Paula did earlier. They had both witnessed Coach in the park, and his subliminal attraction towards people simmering in sorrow. The Makers knew that Coach had his distinctive agenda with his life's purpose. They simply were trying their best to ensure that Coach can see it through. Greg sat and digested all the information that Paula had just disclosed to him.

He regurgitated a familiar question, "If this Jerry is so miserable, how was Coach not attracted to his suffering?"

Paula simpered as she answered, "I thought the same thing on my way home! Frank told me that his parents are abusive and detached from Jerry's life."

"Ah! So, Jerry's pain comes from a different place. More out of anger and fear than it is sorrow." Greg immediately related to this young man's strife.

Greg was raised in a dysfunctional family, as many of us are. His father was a raging alcoholic, and his mother was a depressed pill devotee. This was the era in which these emotional inhibitors were just making their way to the masses. And Greg's mother tried them all, frequently. She was a sweet and frail woman that did her best to keep Greg progressing through his childhood. When Greg's father got intoxicated, Greg's mother would hide her body and her mind. Throughout Greg's teenage years, he would step in to defend his mother from the wrecking ball his father degraded into. He understood young Jerry's situation all too well.

Chapter 12:

The night had come, and Coach was awaking from his selflessly induced coma. When he walked down the hall to see his Maker parents respond to his physical escalation, Coach reacted the only way he knew how. With a bright smile. Coach now looked like a teenage boy, thirteen in age, his pectoral muscles were more pronounced. His jawline was extended and more defined, and his muscles were further toned. Greg and Paula had become amazingly comfortable with this cause and effect structure that Coach's body displayed.

Greg just greeted the young man with a, "You're looking good there, Sport." Not sure what else to do in this situation other than embrace it.

"You must be hungry, Coach. Sit on down at the table, and dinner should be coming up real soon." Paula encouragingly announced to their two-year-old, teenage boy.

Coach could understand and follow orders fine. He could read and process information. Coach could not organically speak or express emotions, other than that original smile of his. Coach carried himself well, his posture was upright and aligned. He adapted well to his ever-altering physique. The only sparsely used forms of communication had been the nodding of his head in affirmation, a fearful shriek as a child, and the tears he let out after Roger left. But this felt like ages ago. Coach primarily just smiled and followed his unique intuition. To the people encountered by Coach's brilliant touch, they did not need any more description of this remarkable soul. To those that only know how to perceive him objectively, he must appear as an oddity.

Paula and Greg knew how society might identify this young man. More directly, they knew how the faculty and students would react to him when he returns to class tomorrow. They just felt like the most appropriate way for them to give back to Coach was to give him a normal life. A life where he can smile and play with other kids, while he is still in kid form. An environment where he can learn and possibly develop more human traits. This was the best that Greg and Paula could offer in their life's present interval.

The new day came with much angst from the Makers. Greg and Paula discussed potential scenarios that could play out upon Coach's return to school. They wrapped up breakfast, reassuring one another that things will be fine.

"Hey, Coach has Frank on his side now." Paula reminded Greg as he put on his jacket before heading off.

"Thank the lord for that. Have a great day everyone, love you both." Greg stated for the morning.

Coach had just gotten new clothes for his first day of school, and they were now one size too small. Paula grabbed one of Greg's shirts to cover Coach's lengthened torso. It looked like he was at least five feet tall now. She was astonished by these wild advancements and had logged her observations down in a journal. Paula took her first measurement of Coach's height after she and Greg witnessed the miracle in the park and the repercussive growth that ensued. Coach came in at four feet and six inches. Today, after Paula took her measurements, Coach was four feet and eleven inches. She did not have enough information to derive any measurable correlation yet, but her curiosity would keep her pursuant.

As Paula drove Coach to school, she did her best to comfort the smiling kid, "If anything happens to you... You go right to Frank or Ms. Plankton."

The car pulled around to the front of the school; children were dispersing through the parking lot and siphoning towards the main entrance. In the flood of kids, Patricia Plankton was standing there waiting. She searched through the swarm of students passing her until her gaze met Paula and Coach in the parking lot. Ms. P had been waiting for Coach's arrival. She was a kind-spirited woman. Paula parked the car, assisted Coach out, and ushered him over towards Ms. P.

"Aren't you looking healthy today, Coach?!" Patricia vociferously announced so the passing waves could hear. "I hope that everything is normal for our Coach here?" as she asked this question, Ms. P examined the developed teenager.

"He is as normal as Coach gets. Please, keep both eyes on him today." Paula exclaimed before returning to her car.

Ms. Plankton escorted Coach to their class so the day's lesson could commence. It was a peaceful morning until lunchtime came around, and Jerry was on the prowl for Coach. Jerry seemed extra fiery today. He had fresh bruises on his forearms where some adult had inappropriately squeezed him. Coach was again the last one out of the classroom horde, and as all the kids scampered to the cafeteria. Coach smiled at Jerry in the hallway again.

"What the fuck are you? Some sorta freak?" Jerry shouted towards Coach before mischievously shoving his left shoulder. Coach returned a smile. He did not know the meaning of anger and violence; he did not understand what was happening.

Around the corner of the hall, Frank heard the rattling commotion as he was replacing a trash bag. The custodian swiftly finished the task at hand and rerouted towards the sounds of a potential skirmish. The closer Frank got to the dilemma, the faster he recognized Jerry's disturbed voice.

Frank finally erupted through the corridor to catch Jerry harassing Coach. He yelled immediately, "Jerry, get your greasy mitts off of that kid!"

Jerry scattered, chuckling along, as he delighted in his efficacy for viciousness.

Frank strolled up to Coach after the bully was out of sight, surprised to see such a bright smile on his face. "Looks like I caught him just in time.

That little shit has a lot of misplaced rage in him." He explained to Coach while accompanying him to the cafeteria.

Coach had once again been the last one to get his lunch. It was fine, though; he did not feel jealous or embarrassed. After his vegetarian sides were plated, Coach sat in the first open spot he found. He sat on the winter cap of a timid and charming girl named Jessica Fasser. She slipped the hat from under Coach without asking him to move. Jessica had been saving this seat for Coach.

"Hello there." Jessica turned her head to the right and greeted Coach.

Coach smiled through the spoonful of green beans and corn kernels he was steadily shoveling into his mouth.

Jessica laughed at the display Coach offered, and abruptly revealed, "I saw what you did to Mr. Frank yesterday."

Coach continued his smiley consumption with no hesitation. He was not capable of concern in any manner, including worrying about who witnesses his turquoise majesty. Jessica quickly realized this as she studied

Coach's demeanor. She was an advanced student, her love for literature and

art started at an adolescent age. Jessica was an only child, both of her

parents worked cryptic jobs she has heard them referred to as 'brokers' and

'agents'. The young girl had learned to thrive independently and observe

her surroundings. What Jess observed yesterday was like nothing she had

ever witnessed in her eleven years of life. The vibrance of the turquoise, the

benevolent transaction of definitive relief, and the compassion. She

witnessed it all. It played out like an artful performance to her, like the

greatest performance she ever watched.

"What are you?" Jessica quietly wondered aloud to herself.

They both finished their lunches and resumed the rest of the day's

lesson. Coach had now become acquainted with Jerry, who Coach would

see grimacing at him whenever he cared to look his way. And Jessica, who

was kind and could be spotted on the other end of the room beaming

admiration towards Coach. Overall, it was a successful and harmless first

full day of school for sweet Coach.

Greg arrived to pick Coach up from school today. He arranged himself at the front walkway with some of the other parents. They chatted amongst one another, exchanging simple pleasantries.

One of the parents welcomed Greg, "Howdy there, Guy. Your face lookin' new 'round this here crew."

Greg was barely focused on what the man was blabbering about as the children poured from the school's agape doors. "Hello, I am Greg Maker. Nice to meet you all." Greg's voice rode a crescendo to introduce himself raucously enough for everyone to hear.

"Which one-these rug rats are yours?" the man inquired.

Greg was feeling alarmed as the wave of children died down, and he did not see Coach's smiling face in the mix. Then, trailing behind the pack assisted by Ms. P, Greg proudly identified the kid by her side.

"That handsome fellow, right there. That is my son. Coach Maker." Greg boasted as Coach smiled his way through the doors.

The two Maker boys met halfway, and Greg could hear the man behind him say, "That boy looks like he a high schooler." The man scoffed after making his impolite comment.

Greg walked past the man and held his disgruntled stare firmly, while he and Coach trudged to the car.

"Bye, Coach!" a bright voice chimed from afar, it was Jessica. Greg waved to the gentle young girl, and Coach directed his smile at her as they pushed onward.

"Making friends, I see." Greg commented as they both entered the car.

Coach was conscious, smiling and leaving the facility with everyone else. Greg was content with the success of today. He instinctually informed Coach about how his day went, about what he does, and the people he helps across the world. Greg is very gratified by his philanthropic career choices. He has worked hard to help create a humane network that provides aide for folks in impoverished countries. Greg's department specializes in educational infrastructure, but he dabbles in all the related sectors.

Greg has had quite a challenging journey through his own life. As a child, growing up in his troubled household environment, Greg had to fend for himself. There was no moral guidance for Greg. His dad was exceedingly inebriated and sadistic throughout his upbringing. His mother was engulfed in fear and regret. While Greg was forced to get a job in his teenage years to buy his own groceries, he also protected his mother from the brutality of his ruthless father. It was a difficult lifestyle for young Greg, but he did his best to get through it.

One high school day, Greg got called to the principal's office, where he was told that his father had mercilessly beaten his mother to death—murdered in cold blood. Greg's foundations were shattered, his heart filled with indignation and he felt only hate for his father. This was the most pivotal point in his developing years. He was bordering a frightening threshold. It took time, support, and strong will but Greg ultimately chose to dedicate his life to helping others in need after this horrendous incident. What has lingered with Greg, even after Coach's exorcism, was his aversion towards murder. After living through his delicate mother's murder, by his father, Greg had formed a confounding-sized trepidation in his heart. The very thought, or association to such a heinous act, traps his mind back in those hopeless moments in his past.

The coincidence with Coach and the house on Harmony Street lingered in Greg's iron-clad memory. Not necessarily the beauty he released unto the world, but the life he may have inadvertently pilfered. "Life is a treasure, a treasure that we are all gifted when we take our first breaths. Some treasures glimmer longer than others, but the length of our individual glimmer is not meant for others to determine." This is Greg's general philosophy on life, and Coach unconsciously tested its resilience. Greg's worst fear is a repeat occurrence under his watch. He could not fathom how he would cope with any more murder.

"Honey, I'm home!" Greg satirically announced as he and Coach entered the house.

"How did our little guy do today?!" Paula responded triumphantly, running to the door to hug both of her boys.

"He is here in one piece, and conscious. So, I think we did quite well. Right, Champ?" Greg soothed his worried wife, and his worried mind, when he proclaimed this report.

This November 18th, 1999 felt like the first 'ordinary' day the refurbished Maker family had composedly enjoyed since forming this union. The evening proceeded in a corresponding fashion. Greg and Paula joked and discussed current events over dinner. Coach smiled and listened. They all sat around the living room afterward and played a board game.

Amid their game, Greg recalled an enjoyable and brief encounter they had with Coach's new friend. "She was adorable, Paula. Smiley like Coach. She had freckles on her cheeks, pigtails, and bangs. She was the epitome of your classic elementary school girl..." Greg was cheesing harder than Coach as he continued, "... And she hollered out 'bye, Coach' as we were heading to the car. It was endearing." Greg finished his snippet and then took a sip of his wine.

Paula felt a tear roll down her cheek. She was thrilled with the story Greg just told and the status of their family unit.

"That is wonderful, Coach. You made a friend already on your second day. I don't think I even did that during my first week of school." Paula's voice trembled with joy. Neither of them spoke much after that, but all three had different sized grins on their faces.

Chapter 13:

The next couple of months performed like clockwork. The Maker family had settled into their routines. Greg and Paula carried on with their noble works. They kept Coach's public time limited. The sweet Coach smiled and progressed through his first two months of school, relatively unscathed. He had Jessica, Ms. Plankton, and Frank all on his team, but Jerry would seize any opportunity he could to annoy Coach. Jessica studied Coach intensely over these couple months, infatuated by his quiet and mystical nature. They had become 'good' friends. Unfortunately, a relationship with Coach is one-sided with emotional support and other social connections. But Coach will be there to listen and smile.

The holidays came and went for the Makers. They kept the celebratory events concise for Coach's sake. Greg had only distant relatives left in his family, individuals he has never met and others he chooses not to communicate with anymore. Paula has one sister and one brother that each reside in different states, so it is always a hassle getting everyone together simultaneously. Since the death of their daughters, Paula has heard little from her family. She does not resent them for it, but she also has not

informed them about Coach either. Coach got to experience Thanksgiving,
Christmas, and the terrifying turn of the millennium. The news was riddled
with frantic and menacing stories of Y2K. Stories of how this changing era
would bring about pandemonium in society's industries and infrastructure.
It did not, at least not at first glance.

A fresh millennium may not have released the immediate and
apocalyptic results that the media predicted, but it did launch the
technological era. The internet was amassing major traction, and social
media was beginning. Nature continued being devoured across the globe at
an alarming rate. These addictive technological devices and programs
proceeded to require copious natural resources. The rapidly increasing
population size perpetually required more resources. The advancing,
globally connected way of commerce proportionately entailed even more
natural resources to function. People continued to manufacture, create,
produce, expel, sell, and consume with no regard for the consequences. The
oceans were filling up with human-generated refuse; ecosystems failed, the
global climate was altering in looming and catastrophic ways. These
worldwide phenomena were transpiring, and the powers that be facilitated

their intensity through a craving for monetary affluence. Decisions were no longer being made for the 'greater good' of the people, let alone the sake of the planet. The year 2000 sparked a radical obliviousness in people. A total disregard for the environment in which we all must reside. Nature must figure out its own way to endure and adapt to its human colleagues' Earthly indifference...

Back in a quiet Tennessee neighborhood, the Maker family was enjoying their vegetable stir-fry and debating on the news reports of impending doom. It was a cold January evening. The news was spewing through the television speakers at a reduced volume. This night, the Maker family was sitting around the table with a guest. Coach's friend, Jessica, had been invited over for dinner by Paula. Greg and Paula want to get acquainted with anyone that is friends with Coach.

"What is your opinion on all of this?" Greg asked Jessica from across the table, referring to the news reports.

She was finishing a mouth full of vegetables before murmuring, "I think a lot of it is unrealistic, all the Y2K silliness. But I do feel like the

Earth could be in serious trouble based on those short stories on climate change."

Paula smiled at Jessica's simple yet insightful response. She and Greg both shared the same outlook. It was a worrisome time. But they had Coach. Coach was repeatedly humming discombobulated tunes, and smiling, while he munched all the way through his plate. After a short continuation of this macro debate, the Maker's cleaned up and Paula took Jessica back to her house.

"What do your parents do, Jessica?" Paula investigated as they slowly approached the sizeable residence.

"They work as representatives or agents for some organization, they never really tell me much. They are not around very often, and rarely are they home together at the same time." Jessica replied in a subdued manner. She thanked Mrs. Maker for dinner, and the ride, and strolled on into her two-story residence.

The next day, back at school, Coach was greeted at the entrance by an energized Jessica Fasser. Coach kept his energy and demeanor at a consistently flat rate, but his smile was always bright and inviting. Jessie placed her arm around her pal while the two made their way to the classroom. The class looked different today, something was missing. When Coach gazed around at his peers, he noticed the absence of a foul smile. Jerry was not in class. Thusly, Coach's day swimmingly persisted. There were no physical confrontations or mishaps on this 25th of January.

The day went so well that Jessie had persuaded her homebound mother to allow the Makers to come over for dinner tonight. Karen Fasser, Jessie's mother, agreed to entertain her daughter's new friends for the evening. Karen was an overburdened CIA agent that respected her work and despised it. She could not speak of the atrocities she has committed and observed. Karen could not get back the time she has spent away from her child, but she could persuade herself that she was helping to accomplish good. Karen has taken numerous lives throughout her career; it is part of the job. That is the ultimate rationalization most agents exploited to maintain their sanity. Mrs. Fasser had reconfigured her character around a life of secrecy. So, she was a skilled performer when in the public eye.

Since each of the Fasser parents were regularly gone and often concurrently. Jessica was mostly raised by their Spanish caretaker, Sofia.

Sofia spoke little English but understood it fluently. She had been with the family since Jessica was born, she is sweet and uncomplicated. Jessie is quite fond of Sofia. Sofia had been more of a mother to Jessica than the absent Karen had been throughout her childhood. Sofia had been abandoned by her father when she was young, she hustled her way into adulthood and met Mr. Fasser when she was eighteen. Karen was pregnant at the time, and Sofia was jobless and desperate. Sofia was a godsend onto the Fasser's disheveled lives. Sofia has lived in one of the four bedrooms in the house ever since before Jessie's birth. Sofia is an integral member of the Fasser family. Tonight, Sofia was making her famous paella for the Maker family.

The sun had not completely set, while the Maker family parked their car outside of the Fasser house. They examined this dual story bungalow with its manicured, green façade, as they ascended the front porch's steps. Greg knocked on the front door, and Jessie was there to greet them.

"Hi, friends!" Jessica welcomed them, each with elation and embrace. Behind her was Sofia, who was introduced to each member of the Maker family.

"Mucho gusto," Paula offered as she greeted Sofia. Sofia's eyes lit up as Paula continued speaking Spanish to her. It was refreshing for Sofia to have a full conversation in her native tongue. Paula and Sofia trailed off through the spacious dining room and into the kitchen as they cackled between their Spanish discussion.

Greg was standing in the vestibule with a bottle of wine in his hand, and he asked Jessie, "Where is your mother, Sweetie?" His eyes wandered around the modern setting and he slowly sauntered through the main floor.

Jessie led the way and exclaimed, "She is probably finishing some work upstairs."

Karen was doing just that in her second-floor office. She had to finish a report required as a preliminary foundation for a vital mission in the Middle East. Her phone was pressed to her ear as she was explaining to Victor, her husband, that their dinner guests have arrived at the house. Karen was harmoniously typing the rest of the report as she caught up with her distant spouse.

Meanwhile, downstairs, Sofia and Paula were in the kitchen exchanging Spanish blows, Greg was following Jessie around the main floor of the house, and Coach was standing still in the entrance of the home. Coach's gaze had diverted upward, towards the second floor of the home, where Karen was hurrying to finish her work. There was something drawing Coach towards the staircase, and he was not one to battle his intuition. The rest of the group were out of sight and Coach had begun to make his way up the stairs. After reaching the top of the steps, Coach was guided into the room occupied by Karen. She continued multitasking as Coach unobtrusively entered the room and approached Karen from the rear.

As Karen finally felt Coach's presence near her, she turned and let out a shriek, "Oh, dear God!" she was startled by his mysterious attendance.

"You must be Coach." Karen iterated after she noticed the young man's sprightly smile and odd mien that Jessica had described to her.

Greg and Paula halted in their discussions as they heard the shriek from upstairs and they each shouted out, "Coach!?"

Before anyone started for the stairs, Coach had placed his curative hand on Karen's back. The process had begun. The turquoise hue immediately, and dazzlingly, radiated from Coach's skin as Karen became paralyzed with transference. While her groans of alleviation heightened, and

Coach's turquoise brightened. The entire dinner group downstairs made their way up in sequence. Greg popped the door open wide so the entire party could get a view of this luminous magnificence. Jessie's eyes welled up.

"Dios mio!" Sofia screamed from behind Jessica. She charged in after Mrs. Fasser, supremely uncertain as to what she was observing. Paula caressed Sofia and gently explained to her that everything would be fine. The sounds of crying and awe saturated the office's air.

"Karen!?! Karen!? What is happening, Babe? Talk to me!" hollering from the corded landline could be heard in between the sounds of reverence. It was Victor, who was still on the line with Karen before Coach laid his hand on her.

The conversion completed. Coach promptly passed out on the floor; his skin tone gradually returned to its humanly olive color. Karen finally snapped back into reality, and Victor screamed for someone to reconcile his worry.

Jessica scurried over to the dial. She frantically grappled with the phone until she replied to her father, "Pops?! Everything is alright, Momma is fine."

"That sure did not sound fine to me. Can you put your mother on? What is going on there?!" Victor's angst had mildly subsided, but he still had a bevy of questions.

Jessica considered her recuperating mother; she expressed to her father that Karen was not ready to talk just yet. While Jessie stayed on the line, Greg picked up Coach's unconscious body and brought him downstairs to the sofa. The fire alarm had just gone off, smoke billowed in the unattended kitchen. Sofia rushed downstairs; Paula braced Karen as she readjusted herself in her desk chair. Paula empathized with the exotic sensations Karen was attempting to process in these moments of recovery.

Victor was demanding answers from his eleven-year-old daughter, answers she could not articulate. Finally, when Karen was acclimated enough. She grabbed the phone from Jessica's inert hand and said to Victor, "I am okay, Vick. I will call you later." Karen swiftly retired the phone to its resting position.

"I think I need a drink." Karen illuminated, and the three ladies made their way down the steps. Paula provided support as Karen was still collecting her sense of balance. Although her physical body took some time to mend, Karen's psyche had never felt brighter.

Karen took a squat on one of the love seats in the living room, adjacent to the dining room, where she squawked a huge sigh of relief.

"Well, I am Karen Fasser... Welcome to our home." Karen's laugh erupted, and the rest of the party joined in as they basked in their incredulous reception.

"Do you need to get that boy to the hospital?!" Karen emphasized, once their collective laugh receded. "Please, tell me that he is going to be fine," she requested from her new acquaintances.

"He will be alright. We are 95 percent sure." Paula confirmed, after looking towards Greg for unconscious approval.

The Makers properly introduced themselves to Karen and did their best to explain what Coach is. They shared their exorcism stories to quell Karen's disorientation. Jessica decided it was as a good time as ever to divulge her Coach experience. Jessie expounded on her viewing of Frank's exorcism to all the adults in the room. They all exchanged admirations and opinions for why Coach does what he does.

"So, Coach is an extraterrestrial being?" Karen invited this notion through her line of questioning. "He is not just human," she stated as a matter of fact. Karen was in the CIA, she analyzed and decoded information for a living. Her tact was correspondent to her education. She felt great respect for Coach, after what he selflessly did for her and others, but Karen analyzed life objectively.

"He may be alien in his uniquely eccentric ways, but I don't feel like he is from the cosmos." Greg expressed his opinion as the discussion stormed on.

Sofia sat next to Jessica, on the edge of her seat, enthralled by the inexplicable content this night brought. Dinner had been ready for an hour now, but they were all immersed in this conversation while Coach rested.

Karen suggested they continue the dialogue over supper, "Sofia, amiga. Can you help the guests get seated at the table, please?" Sofia zipped up and readied the table for her paella.

Greg countered by advocating they take Coach home and reschedule.

"You came here to have dinner. Please, I insist. You must try Sofie's famous paella. She is a superb cook." Karen urged the Makers to stay a while longer.

Paula concurred with Karen, pacifying Greg, "We have seen this process several times now, Honey. Coach will be out for at least a few more hours. He looks like he's sleeping fine where he is."

It was now 8:17 pm when the paella was finally served. The dinner party assembled around the table, Greg opened the bottle of wine he brought and poured the four adults each a glass.

"Jessie, would you like to try a little wine with dinner?" Karen was feeling enriched on this night, more liberal than she has ever felt.

Jessica nodded her head, yes, and Greg poured her a small glass of Pinot Noir. She sampled the robust beverage, making a repulsed face as the fluid washed across her taste buds. All the adults had observed this display and giggled at the predictable result. They feasted together, shared in each other's elegance, and saluted the motionless Coach throughout the meal. The paella had large prong presented on the top, but the rest of the meal was vegetarian, and it was delicious.

Greg lay his fork down on the plate, in surrender, and exalted Sofia, "That was subliminal, My Dear. Superb." Everyone else passionately agreed as the adults finished the second bottle of wine Karen had opened.

"I can see why Jessie likes you all so much, especially that mysterious kid of yours. What an incredible story you have awarded us, truly inconceivable. Yet, it makes sense after what we have all witnessed here tonight and the weight lifted from my soul." Karen confessed before swigging down the last bit of vino.

The thrilling evening ended, and the Makers made their way home. Before they departed, Sofia packed up an extra-large helping of paella for Coach. She told Paula, in Spanish, that Coach deserved so much for the being the special creature he was. Greg carried Coach's teenage body, and Paula graciously accepted the compliments.

"Please, do not hesitate to call on us for anything you all might need." Karen extended this final proposal before shutting the front door.

Greg and Paula had gotten Coach settled in his bed and they proceeded to the bedroom where they made love. Coach arose early the next morning. Greg heard him clunking around in his bedroom. When Greg got up to check on Coach, he was only slightly surprised by Coach's new physique. The most shocking, and latest, attribute was the patchy stubble formulating on Coach's cheeks and under his chin. Greg was instantly excited to teach his boy how to shave. It was something he always longed for.

"Looks like we have an early morning lesson on our hands today, Coach." Greg candidly stated.

Mr. Maker took his illegitimate child to the bathroom so he could provide him a lesson on how to properly shave. They stood side by side, Coach listened and followed directions as he had always done. Coach's smile was broad, like his newly developed shoulders. The young man followed the mature man in his manicuring actions. Greg's smile was as extensive as Coach's, and neither of them knew of the dismay the day would bring.

Chapter 14:

Paula awoke to the sight of the Maker boys shaving together in the mirror's reflection, she smiled to herself and went to prepare pancakes for breakfast. She, too, was no longer shocked by Coach's overnight growth. They had observed the cause and effect enough to anticipate the uncontrollable outcome. Greg and Paula just fretted about the children's reactions at school. "How much longer can we keep him amongst sixth graders?" Paula pondered as she buttered the warmed griddle in front of her.

"Something smells good!" Greg announced as the freshly shaven men shuffled down the hallway together.

"Blueberry pancakes for our special guy." Paula stressed as Coach sat at the table. Greg went to grab a cup of coffee and a kiss from his wife.

They ate their breakfast, recapped the previous night, and Greg offered to drop Coach off at school.

"Should we be taking him right back there after last night?" Paula anxiously asked. Unsure about how to raise this special being.

"Of course, Honey. Coach has multiple people looking out for him. Until last night, he had gone over two months without any episodes." Greg felt confident in the network they have built around their family unit.

Paula shook her head vertically, as Greg made valid points, and retorted, "I suppose you're right, Greggie."

The Maker boys left the house after each receiving a kiss from Paula, and away they disappeared. Paula recorded Coach's height after breakfast, five feet and three inches. These were substantial variances that even kids will notice. Paula's concern profusely returned the more she let her anxiety spread.

"As Greg said, Coach has several folks looking out on his behalf." Paula mollified herself.

Coach was greeted at the front of the school by his established best friend, Jessie. She smiled and waved at Mr. Maker as Coach made his way to her. They went to class, where the intensity of noise was hectic. The kids were in particularly energetic moods today. Coach took his seat and scanned the room, as he traditionally did. He glanced through the sea of smiling faces, from right to left, and landed on Jerry's ominously resentful frown. Jerry had been locked in on Coach since he walked through the door. Jerry's right eye was swollen and purplish-yellow, the colors of a recently planted contusion. There was a scar with fresh stitches on his adolescent jawline. The rest of the class seemed to pay no mind to this beaten kid, and he paid no attention to them—just the smiling Coach across from him.

School was a safer place for Jerry than his own home. They patch young Jerry up when he shows up battered. His parents not only disregard their son's well-being, mentally and physically. But they abusively release their transgressions on him. The cops have been called on these parental figures and they have been jailed. But in this town, it does not take one much to descend back to one's pernicious ways. Especially two ill-willed addicts like the Dingle couple. The school staff members have tried conversating with Mr. and Mrs. Dingle directly when they can get ahold of them. Ms. Plankton has visited the Dingle residence a handful of times to disapprove of their raising of Jerry. The last time she went on their property, she was accosted with a shotgun. The Dingles are the town scum. They are the stain on your countertop that will not abate, no matter what product or apparatus you use. Jerry knew it. Everyone knew it, except for Coach.

It was Recess time, the kids' favorite period. Today, a full hour of recess was granted for the last portion of the day. All the children eagerly followed Ms. Plankton to the playground. It was a crisp, late afternoon, but the sun was still peering through the porous clouds. Ms. Plankton coordinated a game of kickball on the baseball diamond. She was being bombarded by the excited sixth graders. Jessie was athletically inclined and loved competition, so she set Coach up in the outfield with the other insignificant participants. After Jessica got Coach settled on the extensive grasses, Ms. P quickly glanced up to make sure Coach was fine. The gymnastically unconcerned Coach wandered in the open field, disengaged from anything happening in this kickball contest.

While Coach trailed away from the action, he heard imminent snarls mounting more intensely with each passing second. When Coach looked up towards the horizon, he saw Jerry barreling towards him in a blistering rage. Coach did not react, and he did not deviate from his aimless wandering. He just stared at the incensed young man coming his way. Jerry was now within an arm's reach of Coach's serene manner. The bitter Jerry clutched

Coach without hesitation and corralled him to a secluded corner of the playground. The kickball game proceeded in what felt like another land.

"What the fuck are you!?" Jerry screamed into Coach's face, searching for an answer he would not receive. "Answer me, you creepy fuck!"

Coach just smiled in Jerry's face. Not a word or a bit of emotion expressed otherwise.

A second later, Jerry swung a vicious right hook. This punch connected with the left side of Coach's face, knocking him back against the corner of the chain-linked fence. Jerry continued swinging on Coach's unduly advanced body with no regard for his welfare. As he rotated from left to right, body to head, Jerry let out sobs of wrath. Coach was still standing upright when Jerry took a reprieve from his twenty-second spree of alternating blows. Coach was still smiling at Jerry while his face swelled in different areas. Jerry wanted Coach to retaliate, to express fear and vulnerability. He wanted Coach to suffer as he has.

"Hit me, you freak..." Jerry was seething with detestation. "... I hate you!"

It was not Coach that Jerry hated, but his parents for what they have turned him into. He hated his life. Jerry needed to inflict pain on something, something pleasant, something jovial. When Jerry momentarily reflected on this, and then refocused in on Coach's smiling face, he was teeming with antipathy again.

The attacks recommenced, and they were even harder this time. Coach withstood, like Muhammed Ali doing the rope-a-dope, with his back against the fence's corner. Jerry kept his head down and concentrated on beating Coach's torso. After ten consecutive knocks to the core, Coach coughed up a substance with the consistency of blood. At first spray, only a few droplets of blueish-green spatter had dribbled on Coach's chin. Jerry unwittingly persisted in clobbering Coach, regardless. Until Coach spewed a whole mouthful of turquoise blood on him. The blood hit Jerry's forehead and streamed down his face. This caused him to relent his harmful ambition. Jerry felt the plasma stinging his eyes and surging into his mouth.

"You are a disgusting fuck! What the hell is this?!" Jerry gurgled through the blood flowing down his throat.

The furious Jerry frantically tried to wipe the body fluid away from his face, but the back of his left hand stuck to his blood-covered left cheek. Jerry immediately struggled to pull it away with his free hand and felt his skin tearing from his skull. Jerry attempted to screech in pain, but no noise would exit his insulated passageway. He brushed his right hand across his forehead and the two body parts congealed together. Jerry's eyes were glazed with gore, but they were filled with horror. He did not deserve the transformation taking place as much as Coach did not intend for it to happen. Nevertheless, it was occurring.

Jerry's face wilted into a reddish-blue paste that drizzled off his skull. As the multi-colored slime trickled onto his shoulders and torso, they melted through his flesh and bone like molten lava. The turquoise sludge penetrated down through his organs, accumulating mass with every liquefied component. Jerry's frame became porous and feeble, his carcass crumpled in the corner of the playground. After a full two minutes of decomposition, Jerry Dingle was now a burbling heap of brownish mess. His clothes were peppered throughout this muddle, and by the end of the dissolution, Coach felt faint.

Frank was emptying the trash cans, in the dumpsters behind the school, as he had always done. As Frank scanned the surrounding vicinity, in the distance, he detected the end of a scuffle in an isolated corner section of the playground. From the hundred yards away, he reckoned he saw one of the two kids crinkle down into nothing. Frank turned back around to place the evacuated garbage containers down before heading over to check out the situation. While Frank neared the area, he realized it was Coach churning in the soil close by an inexplicably strange burning bush. Around the bush and Coach, were dilapidated fragments of clothes covered in a brownish fluid. Frank did, however, find a recognizable pair of stained Adidas sneakers.

"This is Jerry's garb," Frank thought to himself. He glanced all around the yard to verify there were no spectators. Frank could hear a kickball game going on around the bend of the establishment. The man felt uneasiness in this gloomy corner of the schoolyard. The formidable burning bush was dripping with some vulgarly fresh liquid, as if it had just been showered with this foreign element. The shrub appeared robust though, like it had been thriving in this spot for years. Frank sprinted around the bend to inspect the sixth-grade kickball game, accounting for every student in the class except Jerry. The children and teachers were all distributed around the baseball diamond, submerged in their friendly competition.

Frank was in a moral dilemma now. His instincts were telling him that something awful transpired between Coach and Jerry in that bleak corner, something fatal. The only evidence he had was his fleetingly questionable observation of the end of the quarrel. He was certain there were two indistinct figures, and now there is only one. Frank is a simple man, but he was not daft. He can infer based on what he had viewed in this ambiguous morsel of time and the power he has experienced from Coach. The staff had warned Jerry on frequent occasions, not to harass Coach, but never did they imagine it would end in demise.

Frank felt clammy and nervous. He knew that he must decide one way or the other. Coach had salvaged Frank's life and the life of several others. Francis knew this messiah had more work to do. Frank pledged that he would be Coach's protector, so protect him, he must. After a grueling minute of assessment, Frank had chosen. The custodian sprinted over to the rising Coach. He collected all of Jerry's sullied attire and placed it in a trash bag.

Frank cleared away the peculiar fluid on Coach's upper body, with a rag, and threw it in the bag with Jerry's remains. Just within the two minutes of scurrying around the playground, the odd burning bush had dried of all its dripping fluids. The fluids had not only evaporated, but tiny yellow flowers were squeaking through the deep crimson leaves. It was a dazzling display of pigment and tragedy; a tragedy that only Frank and Coach knew of.

"Coach!?" Frank heard Ms. Plankton calling in the distance, as she started her exploration around the extensive grounds.

"C'mon, Coach. Follow me, Bud." Frank whispered to the now vertical Coach as if someone would hear them in this solemn corner.

Coach and Frank scampered off the school grounds, and to Frank's truck in the faculty parking lot. Recess, and the remainder of the day, was only twenty minutes from ending. In the act of security and apprehension, Frank loaded the bag of evidence and a thrashed Coach into his truck.

"C'mon! C'mon, what do I do?!" Frank mumbled to himself in the stationary truck as he plotted his next move.

Meanwhile, back at the playground. Patricia Plankton had made her way around the yard while intermittently yelling for Coach. She noticed a beautiful, and solitary, burning bush within the grassy corner. It was spectacularly enchanting, "How have I never noticed this splendid plant before?" Patricia broke from her concentration to ponder. When Patricia focused back into reality, she glanced at her watch and returned to gather the kids to prepare their departures. Ms. P stopped one more time on her return track, glared at the marvelous bush, and let out another, "Coach!?"

Chapter 15:

It was now ten minutes until the final bell rang and the children were assembling at the front of the facility. Frank was still in his parked car, panicking through what to do next. He saw a couple of the parental vehicles start filling the parking lot. Frank had not registered the time of day until now. He examined the parking lot hoping to spot one of the Makers. Coach had his head leaned against the passenger window, and his damaged smile still emanated from his bruised face. Precisely at 2:52 pm, eight minutes before school let out. Frank saw Paula Maker pull up into the school's parking lot. He synchronically exited his automobile as Paula parked her car.

Frank fiercely paced through the lot and up to Paula's window. He lightly tapped on the window, and stated, "Good afternoon, Mrs. Maker. I do not want to alarm you or anyone. But Coach is in a bad way. I have him in my truck now and can follow you home if you would please allow it... We need to discuss some things."

Paula saw the sweat accumulating on Frank's forehead and could hear the distress in his anxious tone. "Okay, Frank. Can I see him really quick?!" Paula asked as she finessed her door to get out.

Frank abruptly slammed her door shut and replied through the open window, "I think we should do this privately." His eyes made it abundantly cleared that something severe had materialized.

Paula slipped thru the lot, and Frank followed, she wallowed in concern during the entire eleven-minute drive home. When they both arrived at Paula's, she hastily located her car in a crooked fashion and ruptured from the driver's side.

"Let me see my Coach! I need to see his face," Paula pleaded as she impatiently waited for Frank's truck to cease in the front of the house. She spied Coach's hammered face from the side of her car.

"What is the meaning of this?! WHO did this to him!? Tell me now!" Paula was shouting at Frank from the sidewalk. Frank got out of the car and Paula opened the passenger door for Coach.

As Coach limped his way down from the elevated truck, Paula began to bawl uncontrollably. Frank leaned forward and put Coach's arm around his massive frame to support his walk to the house. Paula rushed to unlock the front door and clear a path for her grimacing teenager. They got Coach positioned on the sofa and then Frank did his best to illuminate the succession of incidents, with the limited information he had. Directly after Frank concluded elaborating, Paula phoned Greg at work to ask him to come home early. Meanwhile, Paula got a warm, soapy cloth to wash Coach's micro-incisions across his face. She despised Jerry for his vicious nature. Frank had not revealed the part about Jerry potentially being a bush now. He thought it best that both parents be present for that news bulletin.

Thirty minutes had passed before they heard Greg pull up in the drive and rush towards the porch. He hastily pushed the door open and studied the ambiance of the room. He feared the worst.

"What in the name of-", Greg reeled off when noticing Coach's injured state.

He was interrupted before he could finish his statement, "Sit down, Honey." Paula morosely uttered.

The four sat together in the living room, Frank reiterated his vague story, but this time he illustrated the burning bush in his revision.

"You never told me about that part!?" Paula curiously exclaimed. "Are you sure you did not just imagine things out there?" She followed up with a question.

"This is far too much for me! Are you saying that Coach potentially turned Jerry into a... Bush?!" Greg was dumbfounded. Yet, it felt eerily like a past affair only he, Coach and the public news were abreast too.

"Jerry had it out for Coach as soon as he was enrolled in the school. I broke up several skirmishes myself. The past month or so, things had successfully calmed down." Frank provided some perspective.

"… I suppose today he broke the streak." Frank finished his contextualizing, with a woeful tone, and hung his head down.

"I don't believe it though! How are we supposed to believe this?!" Greg had gotten up from the couch and began petulantly marching around the room.

Frank temporarily left the family room and went to his car to get the trash bag full of Jerry's stained gear. He sluggishly walked back to the house, uncomfortable with the contents he was holding and the situation he was in. The sun was going down, and Frank felt a chill spring into his bones, he was not sure if it was the meteorological conditions or the predicament causing it. When Frank returned through the front door, Greg and Paula were intensely bickering. They both halted when they noticed Frank had an opaque plastic bag full of something foul-smelling.

"What the hell is that?!" Greg revoltingly proclaimed as the odor pervaded through his nostrils.

Frank reluctantly opened the bag and reached in to grab an article of clothing. He presented the Makers a punctured and encrusted teenager's white shirt. It was coated with a dehydrated, multi-colored element. Brownish-red and turquoise were the predominant colors they could make out. Paula felt a blast of nausea surge from her stomach. The combination of the imagery and scents made her sick, and she galloped away to the bathroom.

Greg felt angst toward Coach, toward another potential murder, and toward losing this troubled boy setting in. When he looked over at the trounced, quasi-child, he felt his love and admiration convert to uncertainty and consternation. Greg's post-traumatic stress of his childhood encroached through his agitated state of mind. He could not stare at Coach's smiling face for longer than three seconds.

"This a disaster! I need a drink... Would you like a drink?" Greg offered to Frank as he tied off the revolting bag of stench and placed it outside on the porch.

"No, thank you. I gave up drinking since Coach saved my life. I was heading down a slippery slope." Frank replied to the proposal and shared a smile with Coach's blemished face.

Paula returned from discharging her lunch, and Greg was manically slamming cupboard doors in search of alcohol. Frank inquired about what else he might do for the family before leaving.

"Burn that bag of vile materials, please, Frank." Paula requested, and hugged the man as he turned towards the door.

Greg overheard Paula's bid from the kitchen and came running into the living room before Frank left. "Should we just be disposing of this child's remains like this?!" he asked, in an outrage, for anyone who cared to entertain the thought.

Frank confusingly glowered at the couple who squabbled again, "How about I leave the bag here for you two to decided what to do with it?" Frank interrupted their fervent argument. "You got nothing to worry about from me. I will not be telling a soul, bye y'all. Goodbye, Coach." Frank shared one more reciprocal smile with his hero as he exited the Maker home.

For the next fifteen minutes, Greg and Paula resumed their argument about how to carry on with Coach. Greg was acting rambunctious and erratic. Paula had not seen this side of Greg surface since they met in college. She knew his history and trauma caused by his coarsely troubled background. Paula also knew of Greg's unalloyed loathing for murder. She just construed this situation differently.

"Look at this boy! Look what Jerry did to him! I don't think he had any other choice. I don't think Coach's mind works, malevolently, like that." Paula persisted in pointing at Coach while she made her case.

Greg could not look at the young man. Something in Greg's chemistry fired spite and resent from his nucleus. He slurred his response. He had consistently made sure there was some brown liquid in his glass, "Well, I think you should know something about Coach..."

As he was on the verge of unburdening his conscience from the vanished soul on Harmony Street, over two months ago. The phone rang, Paula picked up. It was Ms. Plankton on the line. She expressed her concerns about not seeing Coach at the end of the day. Paula suppressed Patricia's worry by assuring her of Coach's safety.

Paula did not disguise her unpleasant attitude, "You really should not be letting kids wander around unsupervised," Paula jabbed at Ms. P's aptitude as an instructor. She had a fire set in her stomach.

Ms. P sounded disparaged through the speaker in Paula's ear, "I am so profoundly sorry, Mrs. Maker. This is not a common practice, I assure you." Patricia affirmed. "The only other kid this happens with is Jerry, but he has regrettable circumstances to contend with. We are not sure about his whereabouts either..." Ms. P unsuspiciously added the last statement as a feeble effort to console Paula.

"No kid should be unattended. But my priority is Coach. Thank you, Ms. P." Paula hung up before allowing Patricia to respond.

Through the duration of that brief conversation, Greg was devouring the bottle of Scotch on the kitchen table. He was irate, mortified, and puzzled. The alcohol was not helping stifle these intense feelings. Greg was not a frequent drinker. Hence, half the bottle of Scotch was getting on top of him.

"Greg, Honey. Please, slow down. Let's talk this through." Paula attempted to calm her mania without the assistance of booze.

"Coach killed a man on Harmony Street! H'was homeless man, but a man," Greg blurted. He could barely string a proper sentence together.

"WHAT!? What are you saying, Greggie? You're not making any sense." Paula was trying her best to soothe Greg as he was pacing around the dinner table with a half-filled glass in hand.

"We nee-inform police, it is right Paul." Greg's lower lip was quivering, his eyes were watering, and he relentlessly strode. Coach observed from the couch, smiling, always smiling.

"Greg, we went over this. Coach won't last in the American penal system. It will destroy him. Let's just ride this storm out like we have several times before..." Paula calmed herself down as she made these statements aloud.

Greg shook his head furiously before struggling to project his faltering voice, "What if-t was our kids?! We wanna know!"

Paula sternly replied, "We would. But this is no ordinary kid that we agreed to foster. He is a special being with a special mission. Honey, we've talked about this. My heart aches for the loss of this boy, Jerry... No matter how wretched he was."

Greg reached for his coat. "Where do you think you are going?!" Paula squealed in a panic.

As Greg clutched the doorknob, he turned over towards Coach one more time. The smile Greg extrapolated from the young man's face, at this moment, set aflame to his entire essence. It was the same smile Coach had always shown, but Greg was abruptly no longer the same man he once was. Greg knew that he could not continue living with this disconcertingly apathetic monster. Greg rashly turned around, kissed his wife on the forehead, grabbed the half-consumed bottle of scotch, and fled to his car before Paula could stop him.

"Greg! Honey, come back!" Paula shouted while scurrying after him, but he peeled away down their street to an unknown terminus.

Paula and Greg have never had a domestic dispute like this in all their years of marriage. Mrs. Maker agonized about her significant other for the rest of the evening, worried over his status and safety. Instead of heading back into the house, Paula grabbed the atrocious bag filled with

Jerry's contaminated relics. She journeyed around to the backyard; Paula would have herself a little bonfire. In any regard, Mrs. Maker figured that it was the inevitable end of this evidence. Then later, when Greg returns, the bag and its contents will be annihilated. Out of sight, out of mind. Paula helped Coach to his bed so he could properly rest. She poured herself a glass of Merlot and stoked a blaze in their stone firepit outside. Once, Paula, had the flames raging, she hurled the entire trash bag into the center of the pit. The smoke from the pit smelled like rancid meat and sulfur. Paula had to retreat inside as the gruesome contents were scorched.

Chapter 16:

The night had taken over the day, on this late January evening, and Greg was recklessly piloting his car on the interstate highway. He swerved through lanes while his mind was drowning in trauma and worry. After a miraculously unscathed drive, Greg instinctually ended up back at his office building. He was unnerved and feverish. Greg grabbed the scotch and stumbled to the front door.

While he battled his key ring and its connection with the lock. He let out a somber, "Fuucck!"

Greg was having a psychological breakdown. He was not composing himself as the calm and gentle man he usually was. The door sailed open and slammed against the wall behind it. Greg did not care if anyone else was in the office, he just knew that he could not go back home. Not tonight. His heart stung as the civil war for morality thundered in his spirit. Greg Maker stumbled his way to his office on the main floor. It was spacious and quaint. The space included a couch he subconsciously intended to sleep on. But Greg knew this night would not allow his mind to rest. Reflectively, Greg worried that he might never find peace again, let alone sleep.

There was no sign of any other personnel in the building, but Greg could barely see straight. The alcohol mixed with a bevy of conflicting emotions had his body disorientated. Greg was too far into his heedless campaign to stop now. He grabbed the empty coffee mug on the desk and filled it up with Scotch. The once warm and inspiring office now felt bitter and apathetic. It was collaged with pictures of villages and individuals that Greg's organization has helped throughout his life's work. Tonight, Greg was disgusted when looking around at these smiling faces. Something about the photographs, combined with his dissolving principles, made his boiling melancholy intensify.

The bottle of Scotch was almost empty, and Greg was beginning to droll on himself in his desk chair. Not even a practically full fifth of booze could silence the turmoil protruding in his mind. Greg glanced over to the picture of his precious Paula on the center of the desk. Tears gushed from his red and glossy eyes. The inescapable truth washed over him, "Coach is a divine being." Greg knew that Coach's time with him and Paula must be only part of his benevolent journey. But as Greg's mind turned down this avenue of thought, he pictured Coach's smiling face. That smile made Greg feel sick to his core. He no longer revered Coach's magnetism and silent grace.

As Greg finished the bottle, he indignantly ripped all his accolades and photos from the walls. Now breathing heavy, and inebriated, Greg sloshed back into his chair. Greg's tears were constantly flowing down his face, and he settled for a minute to ponder. In this moment he had become his father. This was the final straw for Greg. He would not abide by such a parallel.

Greg pulled out a pen and piece of paper to transcribe something. He addressed the letter to Paula.

It read:

My Dearest Love Paula,

You are a person stronger than I. I know that we were gifted a burden and a blessing, but I can no longer live with it. Please, know that my love for you has never faltered. I am certain that you will take care of Coach, and he will take care of you.

Love Forever,

Gregory

Greg left the letter open on his desk for the first person to find his body. He was not a coward at heart, but his mind was fragile and dismantled. Perhaps Coach could use his powers, again, to relieve this agony. But he could never relieve Greg of his memories and his destructive affliction towards murder. Greg knew that Coach would alleviate Paula of her sorrow, though, and that was enough solace for Greg to submit to his end. His frenzied mind could see no other option on this dismal night. Greg

Maker found a spare, cloth, sheet in his storage closet. He shakily climbed

up on his desk to wrangle the eight-foot sheet over the exposed ceiling joist.

While standing on the desk, his neck was only three feet from the beam that

would brace his weight. Greg sloppily tied the two dangling ends of the

sheet together as a makeshift noose. Before the despicable act launched,

Greg reached down to grab the framed picture of Paula. He kissed her still-

posed face and squeezed the frame against his chest. Greg was now

positioned for the deathly dive off the edge of his desk.

He looked at Paula's face one more time and said, "I love you."

Before plunging forward to his expiration.

The Earth was already off to a ghastly start in this year, 2000. It now

had one less charitable soul to fight against the overwhelming tide of

apathy. Greg Maker had committed suicide in his office on the night of

January 26th. His assistant, Tim, had found Greg's lifeless body sagging

from the rafter on the morning of the 27th. The appalled Tim found an

empty bottle of Scotch and a letter written on Greg's desk. Tim immediately

phoned the local police, and subsequently Paula, to inform them both of the

devastation at hand. Tim was directed by the police not to touch anything else in the room. However, Tim immensely admired Greg and would make sure Paula received his final written sentiment.

Paula received a demoralizing call at 7:20 am this January morning. She had finished a bottle of wine to herself the previous night. Paula imbibed herself to sleep on the couch in anticipation of Greg's return. She was startled by the ringing of the phone. She jolted up and over to the buzzing unit in one fluid motion, hoping for a different call. When the news struck her eardrums. Paula dropped the corded earpiece and collapsed to the ground in anguish. Tim was shouting through the speaker as she was hysterically sobbing onto the hardwood floor.

The bruised Coach was roused from his slumber. As Coach rapidly bounced out of bed, he boldly strolled over to Paula's excruciatingly convulsed body on the floor. His hand embraced her back, and his skin turned the luminescent turquoise. Paula had not heard Coach coming. She did not want to be purged without adequately grieving for her husband, but she had no choice now.

The sounds were a profusion of pain and relief exiting Paula's lifeforce. Tim was listening to the noises through the drooping speaker.

After a minute of transference, Paula no longer mourned her recently extinct husband. Paula lifted herself off the ground, thanked the bewildered Tim for notifying her about Greg, and hung up the phone. Coach had traded positions with Paula and was now unconscious on the floor. Residual tears were still cascading from Paula's eyes, and she did her best to haul Coach's battered carcass onto the couch tenderly. Coach was well over 100 pounds now, and tomorrow, or perhaps even later this evening, he will be even heavier.

The cops showed up at the scene of Greg's death. The news reporters followed, and the public was informed of this unfortunate event less than twelve hours after its occurrence. Tim drove over to check on Paula and deliver Greg's last declaration. He was enormously curious about the sounds he had heard during the phone call this morning. When he arrived at the Maker's door, he was astonished to see Paula smiling and cheerful. It was early afternoon, and this woman had just been informed of her husband's suicide six hours ago. As Tim was welcomed into the domicile, he noticed a bruised and lethargic young man on the sofa.

"That must be Coach?" Tim passively asked Paula as she poured him a cup of coffee.

"It certainly is," Paula assured Tim, handing him the warm beverage. "When can I see Greg?!" Paula followed up with the question.

"We thought you would have already made your way down to the morgue. Is everything okay here, Paula... You seem mighty, calm and collected, considering the circumstance?" Tim curiously probed.

Paula felt her eyes swell, "I am using every bit of strength in my being to keep it together, Tim. What the fuck do you want to see from me?" she harshly retorted before taking a sip.

"You are right. I don't know what I was expecting. This is uncharted territory for all of us. No one thought Greg would ever kill himself... He left this letter for you." Tim conceded and reached into his pocket for the letter Greg wrote to Paula.

She read the text several times while Tim observed her, and it initiated another spell of uncontainable tears. "Thank you for coming by

Tim, but could you please leave us to process all of this?" Paula gently requested.

"Of course, Paula. You know I adored Greg, just wanted to make sure you were still standing. And make sure you got this letter." Tim finished his cup of java and made his way to the door.

"Hey. What was all that noise I heard on the phone this morning? It didn't sound like anything I've ever heard before." Tim queried one last time as he reevaluated the young man on the couch.

"If you ever lose your significant other... I will call to hear how you sound, Tim." Paula callously concluded the conversation.

Tim knew he had overstayed his welcome. Once his face hit the atmosphere, the hollering of reports drifted in from the street. There were several local news vans and a handful of reports aspiring for an interview with Paula. She grabbed Tim back into the house, pleading for him to dispose of them.

"Please get rid of them, Tim. I can't handle this today." Paula implored Tim to diffuse this situation on her and Greg's behalf. Tim agreed and fired out to the street to deter these jackals from disturbing a newly anguished widow.

The news ensemble eventually disbanded, and Paula remained in her home for the day. "Greg is not going anywhere. Why do I need to rush to view his corpse?" Paula thought as she pitilessly conducted her daily routines. The sorrow had been stricken from her perspective by Coach, the rest seemed selfish on Greg's part. Paula loved, and always would love, Greg. But his sole decision has left her and Coach by themselves.

The phone was perpetually ringing. Paula answered calls, but repeating the story only solidified her discontent about Greg's choice. She was not embittered, and she was not distraught. Paula knew that she must carry on for Coach's sake. All of Paula and Coach's network of friends and family called to share their condolences. The afternoon was consumed by repeated phone conversations, and Paula had grown weary.

Mrs. Maker was awoken from a nap, on the couch opposite of Coach, by a soft knocking on the front door. She sluggishly lifted herself and glanced at Coach's still frame as she made her route to answer the inquiry. To Paula's delight, she was greeted by Karen and Jessie with warm smiles and a vegetable casserole.

"Hello, sweet ladies. It is so good to see your kind faces." Paula waved the Fasser girls into her home. Mrs. Maker placed the casserole into the oven immediately. She was starved.

Paula gracefully lamented at the table with Karen and Jessie. They discussed what happened the previous day. Karen's face was mystified, and she spoke on the first notion that came to mind, "Jess told me that Coach disappeared from their kickball game at school. We had no idea it unfolded into all of that."

"No one did, not even me. I got the call about Greg this morning. Coach came right up to my suffering and sucked it from my being. That's why he is passed out still." Paula replied to Karen's confusion.

The casserole was ready after they rehashed the spiral of events for over an hour. Karen and Paula continued discussing while Jessica sat next to Coach in the living room. Jessie was concerned for her friend. His face was a handful of colors, not including turquoise. She was summoned back to the dinner table, by Karen, so they could all dine together. Karen changed the topic of conversation because she could see Paula was exhausted from it all.

After clearing her mouth, Karen finished explaining her change of heart in life, "Immediately after my encounter with Coach, the other night. I decided it was time to change my career." Karen was referring to her involvement in secret, and lethal, CIA operations. But she disclosed no details about that.

Karen summarized, "It is time for me to do some actual good in this world."

Paula was uncertain as to what Karen even did for a living, but she was too fatigued to delve into that tonight. Paula replied, "I'm glad to hear that, Karen." She tried to force a smile on her drowsily woeful face. Karen had developed proficiencies in reading situations and people. She knew they should take their leave. Karen helped Paula cleared the table. Mrs. Fasser offered her ear or services for anything Paula, or Coach may need. The Fasser gals made it to the door, during which, Jessie pleaded with her mother to stay with Coach tonight.

"I want to stay with Coach! He has been through so much in these past two days." Jessie overtly begged both adults.

"Mrs. Maker has been through a lot as well, Jess. I don't think that is such a good idea tonight," Karen advised her daughter.

Jessica was weeping as she was being forced to leave. Paula halted them, "It is fine with me if she stays, Karen." Her voice encouraged Karen to allow it.

"You sure, Sweetie? You have had enough troubles today." Karen stated the obvious.

"Jess is no trouble at all. It'll be good to have another pair of eyes on Coach tonight because mine are drained." Paula let out one chuckle after ensuring Karen.

It was Thursday night, but Karen agreed anyway. She offered one more string of condolences before leaving. Paula set up a movie in the living room for Jessica and her to watch next to the sleeping Coach. She moved the loveseat around so Jessie could lie next to Coach, undisturbed. Both of the ladies fell fast asleep in the living room.

Chapter 17:

The time was 2:22 am when Coach abruptly rose from the sofa and opened the front door. The squeaking of the hinges slightly provoked Jess and Paula in the living room, and Coach sauntered through the doorway. He was a man on an unknown mission. His intuition took control of his navigation. It was another one of Coach's pseudo-sleepwalking episodes. This time, he headed the opposite way of Harmony Street. Coach was barefoot, bruised, and striding into the brisk winter air.

Coach was nearly down the Maker's long street before Jessica was awoken by a stiff breeze drafting through the wide-open entrance. Jessie was alarmed by Coach's absence and ran outside to see if she could spot him. Far down the road, she saw Coach determinedly galivanting straight-forward. Jessica grabbed her coat and sprinted after his entranced physique.

When Jessica left the Maker's house, she hurriedly closed the door behind her. This distinct slamming of the door woke Paula from her uncomfortably positioned slumber. She felt sheer panic by the initial sight of Coach and Jessica's absences. Paula swung her coat across her back and charged out into the street.

All three participants, in the Maker household sleepover, were now rushing down the dim and tranquil street. After seventeen minutes of pacing, Coach had slowed down at an abandoned manufacturing plant. This place was shortly over a mile outside of the Maker's neighborhood. The space consisted of deserted and polluted earth. The city shut the plant down over six years ago due to high levels of mercury, lead, and other heavy metal byproducts that poisoned the ground. Coach had stepped onto the massive property, instantly feeling that fiery sting through his feet. He felt the spurts of nausea accruing in the depths of his stomach. This earth was foul, and the contaminates were concentrated. Coach continued to walk amongst the tainted surface, his nausea and pain growing with every step.

There were no civilians, only abandoned neighborhoods. People were forced to migrate from their homes because of the extreme levels of toxins. A total disregard for environmental repercussions, coupled with the profit-centric mentalities of capitalism, have generated a multitude of blighted areas such as this one Coach was on. Jessie and Paula had finally caught up to Coach, he was fifty yards into the estate and gingerly pacing forward.

Paula called out to him, "Coach! Coach, we are here!"

Coach could not acknowledge this call. He was preparing himself for a miraculous release unto this infected land. His body hunched; his internal accumulation was passing its capacity. He opened his mouth and ejected. Out came a girthy stream of turquoise muck sprinkled with spores and exotic matter. A river cascaded from his gaping orifice and spread around this desolate earth for numerous yards. As his projection surged, Coach swiveled his head to cover a more lateral area. The outpour lasted two full minutes until a 500 square foot area had stretched across the ground in front of him. What appeared next was a miracle.

This area of land was deemed uninhabitable, as far back as Paula could recall. Paula and Jessie stood at the perimeter of the acreage while they gazed in awe at the wondrous emergence of vegetation. The land was dusty, russet in color, and lifeless, not even five minutes prior. It was now teeming with bustling nature, lush greenery, and vitality. Jessie and Paula's eyes were distended from their skulls as they watched magic materialize before them. The vines were covering multiple yards of the area in a matter of seconds. Dense patches of ferns sprang from the turquoise muck, they reached up to five feet in an instant. Trees had progressed through 60 years

of a lifecycle, in less than a minute. Flowers, grasses, bushes, weeds,

numerous varieties of foliage came to life.

Both Jessie and Paula were shedding tears of veneration at what they

had the fortune of witnessing. More than a few minutes passed before

Paula's eyes diverted to the, yet again, physically tapped Coach. From

Paula's vantage point, the environmental messiah appeared to get

smothered by the inundation of plant life. She rushed into the grandeur of

flora as its development was culminating. When she got to Coach, he was

surrounded by thick, towering grasses. To her surprise, his inert body-vessel

was lying atop a soft and elevated moss, perfectly caressing his figure.

Coach was out cold. The liberation of whatever ballooned up inside of him

had rendered him unconscious.

Paula whistled after Jessica still patiently waiting by the fence line,

per Mrs. Maker's instructions. Once Jessie heard the call to action, she

sprinted over to where she had remembered seeing Paula enter. The foliage

was so verdant that an onlooker could identify no one from outside the sea

of green.

Mrs. Maker had Coach's flaccid head propped up and directed Jessie once she arrived, "Listen, Sweetie, we need to get Coach out of here. But he is too big to carry all the way home. You stay here in the brush with him, and I will return with the car." Paula darted off back home when she got an affirmative nod from Jessica.

While Jessie sat, holding Coach, she gawped at his uniqueness. Jessica was fascinated with Coach before this scene. Now she is enamored. The moss they were resting on was softer than memory foam and smoother than silk.

"My God, Coach... This is amazing." She breathlessly proclaimed as she ran her hand across the sensational moss. "You are amazing." She continued to endorse Coach after all that she has gotten to study of him.

Roughly forty minutes amassed before Jessica could hear that same whistle in the distance. Paula revisited the magical plot of the forest that Coach and Jessie were stationed in. Paula beseeched Jessie to assist in transporting Coach to the car.

"You grab the legs. I will get his torso." Paula directed the young woman as the two of them grappled with Coach's hefty body.

They kept Coach elevated enough during the transition to the vehicle. Jessie dropped Coach's legs several times along the way but swiftly recaptured them without hesitation. They had the Eco-friendly conjuror packed into the back seat of the car. Jessie turned around to peer through the rear window, one more time, to absorb the beauty Coach had created tonight. The car departed from the site, and the landscaping was just as stunning from Jessica's fading viewpoint.

Paula backed the car into the driveway to save the girls some hassle. It was now past four am when Coach Maker was being hauled back into his residence. Paula did most of the lifting, but the young Jessica exerted enough physical force. The disheveled ladies dragged Coach back to his bed, Paula cleaned off the caked traces of turquoise fluid on his chin, and they both assisted in disrobing him.

"Wow, I am still reeling over what we just saw..." Paula unleashed her delight in a shocked voice, as the two girls sat back in the living room.

"... Coach is incredible. I knew there had to be something more to him!" Jessica replied, acknowledging the effect brought on by the cause of Coach's gift.

"That manufacturing plant has been barren for years. There were hazard signs all along the fences. It should be impossible for vegetation to exist in such a place," Paula began thinking out loud. "I knew Coach had a higher calling."

Both of the women shared theories and speculations as to what, and where, Coach's real purpose is on this Earth. It was devised that maybe Coach was not human. He did not speak, express emotions, fight, hate, explain, complain, or convey the other human behaviors. So far, Paula has seen Coach allow tears to fall from his eyes over Roger's separation. But the young boy did not seem sad. He kept a smile on his face the whole time.

"Perhaps he was tenderly displaying his abilities to Greg and me," Paula pondered as her and Jessica's conversation continued.

For several flashes, Paula recalled the sprouts that formed from Coach's fallen tears. But then she also recollected her and Greg being too awestruck, by the easing Coach granted them, to comprehend the correlation. Paula recanted the aftermath on Harmony Street that Greg exhibited to her. But maybe she was still relishing in her newly refreshed perspective in life. Therefore, neither Paula nor Greg attempted to link how

Coach could have done such a magnificent thing. After actually witnessing Coach's peculiar antics, on this early morning, Paula was enlightened enough to put the limited and unusual pieces together. She logged all the information in her journal.

The rest of the morn passed, and the two girls had finally finished exchanging appreciations and conjectures about Coach. No sleep was had for the rest of the morning. The clock read 7:04 am when Sofia came to the door to retrieve Jessica for school. Jessie tried to argue her way out of going, but both adults insisted that she continue her academic progress.

Paula and Jessica tightly clutched one another, and Jessie said, "Don't worry, I won't tell anyone." The young woman hopped to the car with Sofia.

Chapter: 18

Paula closed the front door and took a deep sigh of reprieve from the whirlwind of contemplations swooshing through her head. She knew that she had to take care of funeral arrangements for Greg today. Paula waddled her fatigued body to the kitchen to start a pot of coffee. Down the hallway came an expanded Coach, his footsteps were louder than ever before. Coach peered around the corner to connect his smile with Paula in the kitchen.

"There's my strapping young man! Coach, go ahead and take a seat at the table." Paula directed Coach with a returned smile, pouring herself a mug of coffee.

Coach followed her directions. He only had on a pair of skin-tight briefs ready to rip at the seams. The young man was now five feet and eight inches after his latest transformation. A sparse, five o'clock, shadow had formed on his face. His legs and underarms were covered with thick, coarse hairs. Coach had long, dark brown hair that symmetrically reached his ears. His teeth had rapidly formed straight, his eyes were a vivid green, and his muscular figure was slender. Coach was a handsome young man that could now fit in most of Greg's clothing.

"You have got to be hungry after all that you vomited up last night, eh, Coach?!" Paula made herself laugh with this one. She chortled away while preparing Coach a grand breakfast.

The phone began its onslaught of ringing by 8:30 am. The first call Paula picked up was from Ms. Plankton; she inquired about Coach's health and whether or not he would be making it back to school soon.

"I am not sure yet, Patricia. He definitely will not be making it back this week. Thank you for calling," Paula hastily retorted and then hung up.

Paula got on with the funeral proceedings. "The sooner I get it done, the sooner it will be over," Paula repeated to herself until she eventually left the house.

There was only one, Channel 2, news van outside when Paula rushed Coach to the car so they could classify Greg's body. Everything went as smoothly as expected. Paula answered the questions from the police, identified the body, coordinated Greg's cremation, and returned home. Paula always remembered Greg's vindication of how he would like to be handled after his death. Greg's spouse kept the affair short and intimate. Only folks that Coach has salvaged were to join the ceremony.

That Saturday, January 29th, 2000, Greg Maker was cremated. He was supported by his wife, Coach, Frank, Karen, and Jessica; everyone showed up frowning except Coach. They gathered in the parking lot of the crematorium before heading inside. Paula had not publicized this event because of the outrageous press it would incessantly elicit. Besides, the media appeared to be busy this weekend. They were covering the miraculously green renovation of the tainted manufacturing plant just outside of town. As the Maker procession walked inside the building together, each attendee was attempting to further soothe Paula in her remarkably calm state.

Coach was in the back of the pack, and he was instantly drawn to an unidentified office in the building. When he jutted through the office doorway, unannounced, he saw a miserable old man weeping into his faded hands. The man was the head warden at this facility for the dead. He had enabled the smoldering of decades of dead bodies, some of whom were his own family. The job had become the man's life, and inevitably his death too. Over the past ten years, he had frequent bouts of sorrows for what his natural life entailed. The necessity versus hate for his career tormented the old man on a nightly basis.

The geriatric man looked up from his moist palms to see a young man marching towards him. "Hello, Young Man. How can I hel-." the old man could not finish his inquiry before Coach had paralyzed his skeleton.

Coach's membrane cast its glorious turquoise glow, and the assortment of noises poured from the grief-stricken old man. The Maker group had not been inside the building for more than a minute before Coach was subconsciously relieving another helpless soul. Coach cannot prevent his gravitational pull towards the miserably downtrodden. Coach was not aware of the ramifications of his actions, or the results that occur after he has gathered this mortal sadness. He simply does what he does. The world needs Coach and more creatures like Coach.

"Coach!?" Paula barked as she heard the familiar sounds of Coach's exorcisms.

The entire group ran with Paula as they followed the groans of emotional exoneration. Paula captured Coach in his turquoise state and screamed out, "No! Coach!?" Some intense maternal instincts kicked in. Paula worried about Coach being 'used up' too fast. When Paula attempted to disconnect the transference, she felt an extreme shock of current burst through her hand momentarily gripped on Coach's turquoise bicep. The old man moaned while the Maker company viewed from the doorway. Coach's shine subsided, and he fell to the floor.

Once the old man came to, he charmingly pronounced, "My dear God, what just happened?! Why do I feel so splendid?!"

Frank shoveled up Coach from the office's ground. The rest of the gang led the elderly man to the spacious and quiet lobby, where they elaborated on Coach's ability. Jessica and Paula shared a smile when Karen concluded her description with, "... And that's all we know about him so far, right, Paula?"

"Right." Paula fibbed, she figured it was probably best she limits the exposure pertaining to Coach's regurgitative ways.

The old man did not speak a word, just sat with his hand propped across his lips, and his elbow rested on his knee. He processed all the information just revealed and factored in his exuberant state. The old man could only think to say, "That young man certainly is a miracle. I think I am done burning bodies. Thank him kindly for me, please." The old man strolled out of the building without another word spoken, got into his car, and rode off to exploit his remaining time on Earth.

"Well... Coach saves another soul." Frank broke the silence in the lobby, hoping to lighten the mood. But they all remembered where they were. It was not a comedic setting.

The crematorium was an empty and bleak place. No one else was working here on a Saturday. Thankfully, the visiting crew included Frank; he was a man of many talents and strengths. The old man had arranged their purchased urn near Greg's covered corpse. Mr. Maker's mortal shell was on top of the conveyer belt leading into the furnace. Paula spoke a few words on Greg's behalf. She then tossed the suicide note Greg had written her on top of his cadaver. Greg's shell was turned to ash, and Frank made his tidiest efforts at collecting the remains.

Frank brought Coach to Paula's car while she carried the urn. Each of Paula's guests clasped and comforted her before they dispersed their separate ways. Frank followed Paula to her house to assist with relocating Coach to his mattress.

Once Coach was positioned, Paula offered to the departing Frank. "Hey, Frank. Would you like a drink? It's been one hell of a week." She began opening a bottle of wine before he answered.

"I do not drink anymore, but I can keep you company if you'd like." Frank agreed to stay for a bit.

"That is right. I'm sorry for the insensitivity, but I will be drinking this whole bottle tonight." Paula confessed aloud as she poured herself a hefty glass of red. Just because there was no longer anguish in Paula's heart, did not mean she was not enduring a plethora of other emotions. Paula vented for a while, and Frank actively listened to her concerns.

"What about Jerry? Have the cops started investigating that scenario?" Paula shifted topics to more pertinent matters.

"Not one bit of care has been spent on that poor boy. Aside from Ms. Plankton, I have not heard a single person even speak his name. Jerry's parents probably don't even know he's missing. They are degenerate folk," Frank solemnly responded.

"That is a damn shame. But also, a relief. If I can be so bold... For Coach's sake," Paula unequivocally stated.

"I feel where you're coming from, Paula. People will just assume that Jerry is inevitably lost in his parents' corrupt lifestyle." Frank was sad talking about the perished boy. He tried to focus back in on Coach, soliciting Paula, "Will we be seeing Coach back at school, Monday?!"

"Not so sure that is a good idea, Frank. Coach will be damn near six feet tall by tomorrow! How am I supposed to explain that to the members of the school?!" Paula implored Frank as she adamantly poured her second glass of wine.

"You don't have to worry about that. The other kids know he is special. Coach brings joy to everyone else in the school. Ms. P and I will continue to watch over him." Frank made his case for Coach's return to the educational realm until he saw Paula's repulsed face.

Paula angrily countered Frank's last statement, "YOU and MS. P watch over COACH?!? Where were YOU when Coach was getting pounded by Jerry? Where was PATRICIA?! How can I trust either of you to preserve Coach?!" Paula followed that rageful line of questioning with the chugging of her Merlot.

Frank calmly answered and continued to argue for Coach's reinstatement in the institute. Frank acknowledged his lapse in protective obligations and explained how Jerry was the only bully in the school. The only kid that ever caused a problem for Coach or others. The case Frank made, for Coach's return, was compelling. Paula agreed to reflect on it throughout the rest of the weekend. She thanked Frank for his camaraderie and dialogue, then escorted him out to the porch. Paula subsequently nestled into the vacant couch and promptly guzzled the rest of the night away.

Chapter 19:

Paula's Sunday morning initiated with a towering and nude Coach smiling over her horizontal body. Most of Coach's bruises along his body had healed. His oddly developed genitalia was right in Paula's line of sight when she turned her head. She noticed the receding testicles. They appeared almost non-existent like he was not meant to procreate with the hominid species. Mrs. Maker shook off her mild hangover, and soared from the couch, after awkwardly examining Coach's strange private parts.

"Let's get you dressed, Honey." Paula guided the naked man-boy-prodigy to her room to pick out some of Greg's clothes. When they passed Coach's open sleeping quarters, Paula spotted the tattered apparel scattered on the floor. He must have ripped it off this morning to avoid strangulation. Coach was recorded, by Paula, at precisely six-foot-tall on this 30th of January. After merely two and a half months, Coach's physique had evolved from a five-year-old adolescent to a twenty-year-old adult.

Paula was ecstatic to see the blueish-yellow marks on Coach's face and body nearly dissipated. She stopped trying to correlate every idiosyncrasy with Coach's majesty. Paula was purely glad to see Coach conscious again. It felt like he had been dormant for the greater portion of this past week. After recapping the brief timeline that Paula had inscribed in her journal, she was astounded by Coach's condensed evolution.

Paula's amazement rapidly turned into unsettlement as she deliberated, "Shit! At this rate, Coach will be over 85 years old by the end of the year!"

Coach grinned at Paula as she envisioned him declining into an older man in less than twelve months. The thoughts made her sob. Paula felt a vivacity and clairvoyance about protecting Coach for the intervening future. She was not sure how long, or from what exactly, she was supposed to defend him. But Paula revealed, to herself, this was her aim now. Not to say that her and Greg's intentions from the start were to do otherwise.

Paula spent the rest of the Sunday afternoon catching up on international news. She read of catastrophic pollution rates, the ruthless deforestation occurring across the world and the islands of plastic refuse in the oceans. She moved onto stories of increasingly toxic chemicals flowing into our natural waterways and the steady upswing of global thawing. She deduced that the turn of the millennium has only amplified humanity's negligence towards its effect on the planet. Scientists, and scholars, warned of the immediate and future ramifications of humanity's negative influences on the Earth's atmosphere. But they also petitioned people to act now in the year 2000. After updating herself, Paula felt that the ascent of technology and the widespread availability of information would ultimately aide humanity in the fight against its downfall.

Paula stepped away from her desktop computer and turned off the news on the TV. It was almost six pm. Coach had been peacefully sitting on the sofa, listening in the entire time, and smiling away at nothing. The alarming news flash of impending doom left Paula feeling queasy, but she knew that they must both eat some dinner. Paula made pasta for tonight. She consumed one bowl, while Coach slurped down the remaining pound of noodles. He gobbled down each refilled plate of pasta with the passion of a thousand Gods. The contemporary Maker duo fell asleep shortly after dinner.

On Monday, the 31st of January. Paula woke with peace in her heart. Coach was finally granted a regular night of sleep. His erratic body was virtually healed, and his smirk was brighter than ever. While she prepared them both breakfast in the early am, Paula contemplated her and Frank's conversation the other night. While processing through this turbulent past week, Paula reassessed Coach's activities. She postulated that Coach has not veered from his Coach ways. He was surviving like the rest of us. Paula desired to be certain about Coach's intentions in disintegrating Jerry, or why he insisted on absorbing the suffering from every individual he crossed paths with. But ultimately, Paula concluded that Coach was doing what he was propagated to do.

"Why keep you from those individuals you make happy then, Coach?" Paula rhetorically asked Coach as he was finishing his cereal.

The widow Maker had decided to grant the school one more chance with Coach. Paula had herself almost completely convinced this was the best option for him. They both packed into the car and headed on over to the school. Paula pointlessly reeled off safety guidelines, personal instructions, warnings, and encouragement to the transcendently abnormal Coach. She knew that Coach would continue following his own biological set of rules. Thus, Paula asserted most of these statements for her peace of mind.

The car ride concluded in front of the school, where there was a barrage of paparazzi, concerned parents, and curious neighbors. Paula wanted to drive straight thru and back to their home, but she discerned that she would have to face the music eventually. Paula left Coach in the car, parked ten yards away, and meandered up to the mob of chattering personnel. Curious questions and desperate demands were being spouted at the perceivably mourning widow.

"Your husband was renowned as a charitable pillar in the community. What would make him want to take his own life?!" one reporter crassly shouted.

"That kid looks like a man! What kind of strange boy you raisin'?!" one of the curious parents bellowed from the middle of the pack.

"There have been some natural phenomena occurring in the metro area. Some of the locals associate this with the arrival of your new son. Care to comment?!" another reported shouted into the mix of babble.

It was pandemonium. There were stirring talks of Coach's eccentricity, Greg's spontaneous suicide, and communal concerns about this exotic boy. The word had gotten out, and the gossip spread like a wildfire. Still, there was no mention of poor Jerry or any concerns of his whereabouts. Paula took the ambush of obscene questions for a minute before responding.

"All I have to say is... I love my dearly departed husband, and I love my special boy, Coach." Paula kept her initial statement brief.

The chaotically ravenous horde of interrogators were not satiated with this mundane response. There was an uproar of outrage and more aggressive questioning. Patricia Plankton scurried over to support Paula as she seemed stunned by the overwhelming attack.

"Please, let this poor woman breathe! She just lost her husband! Do not be insensitive and uncivilized animals!" Ms. P shouted at the vicious swarm on Paula's behalf.

Patricia turned her head and spoke softly into Paula's ear, "I am so sorry. I should have called you to warn you about this. I did not think you were bringing Coach back to school today. These scoundrels have been outside every morning since last Thursday."

This scene had dispirited Paula's hope to allot Coach a relatively 'normal' and social upbringing. She withstood another minute of vigorous and entwined interrogation. Paula shook her head in disgust at the mercilessly constant flood of questions yanking away at her fibers. She took a solitary moment to turn back and soak up Coach's sustaining smile from the passenger seat of the car. At this moment, Paula recollected what her life's objective was now. Support Coach to his future destination. No matter the sacrifices. The school was no longer a conducive environment for such a cause.

"Ladies and gentlemen!" Paula hollered to get the crowd's attention "... My son and I have been through far too much to be subjected to this unruly reactivity. Greg is at peace. Now, the two of us want peace." She braced for a moment while the tears formulated in her eyes. "I will maintain Coach's educational progress at home from now on. Please, do not bother our dwelling and lives. We shall not bother yours. Thank you."

Paula hugged Patricia and diverted back to her car. As she was walking, two of the news reporters followed her. From the outer edge of the group came Frank to halt the reporters' pursuit of Mrs. Maker.

"Let's just let it be," Frank courageously said while presenting his outstretched palms to urge the reporters' relent. Frank turned his head around to wink at Paula and Coach.

The Maker duo departed from the school for one last time. The six-foot Coach was passively sitting in that same seat and smiling for what could be perceived as personal bliss. Pondering throughout the ride, Paula had recognized that Coach does not organically convey human emotion.

"Then, why the ceaseless smile? Why no other emotions?" Paula thought to herself between observational glances at Coach. It was as if some mystical dynamism was guarding Coach and steering him towards his fate. Paula knew that she would now have ample time to analyze the domains of Coach's features.

Paula cruised home, confident in her choice to homeschool Coach. She made calls to her charities, and other associative organizations, about her changes in life structure. Paula notified every single person she could think of, informing them of her future intentions regarding Coach. The wave of exquisite motivation propelled Paula to complete her outstanding tasks. She cleaned the house which had been disregarded for over a week and buried the ashes of poor Jerry's remains out back. Paula gazed over at Greg's urn, and she was inspired to leave the house once more. It was essential to Paula she only focus on what's in store for her and Coach. Paula was zealous about her mission to purposefully, and independently, nurture Coach for the provisional future. To do this successfully, she must eradicate any emotional hindrances.

Paula and Coach took a serene and lengthy ride to the Mississippi River, where she scattered her husband's vestiges. Paula thought this to be the most symbolic resting place for a man like Greg. A man that put his heart into his humanitarian deeds throughout the vast lands on planet Earth. It was only right that he be distributed throughout the bodies of water that provide this globe with life. The Maker pair completed this ceremonial mission and silently boarded into the vehicle for the journey back home.

"It's just you and I now, Coach." Paula smilingly corroborated with her prodigy as she put the car into drive.

From that day forward, it was the Paula and Coach show. Paula provided five to six hours of academic lessons each day, Monday thru Friday. This kept Paula entertained as much as it did Coach, he was an astute pupil. Although Coach could not incorporate opinion into any of his works, he could read, comprehend, and apply knowledge akin to some of the most eminent scholars in the world. Paula was astonished by his accelerated intellect. She strove to pry out any bit of verbal interaction she could from Coach, but it was not feasible. Coach impeccably smiled, nodded, and followed instructions, though. They both stuck to their vegetarian diets, and Paula limited their amount of television interludes. She observed, and documented, all of Coach's attributes and progressions through this phase of time together.

Chapter 20:

Years sprinted by, and Coach was aging like a 'normal' human. Paula was strict about Coach's exposure to society. Throughout these eight years, she only allowed visitation from a handful of entities. Among them were Karen, Jessica, Frank, and Patricia. Paula's family members had visited and encountered Coach during the Christmas of 2002. The evening ended with a dispute about Paula's uncharacteristically secluded way of life. Disgruntled words were exchanged between Paula and her siblings, who only wanted the best for her. Paula explained this was her life now, and they can leave her alone if they do not agree with it. They ultimately chose to do that.

While Coach was being cultivated at home, under Paula's supervision, Jessica had maintained and developed her infatuation with him. Jessie went to the Maker house every day that Paula would allow it, which was several times a week. Young miss Fasser would share stories of her fleeting trials and tribulations to an invulnerable Coach. She liked to believe that her stories resonated with him. They did not, but he involuntarily beamed at her anyway. Jessica confessed her unusual love for Coach when she had reached the eleventh grade and blossomed into a beautiful young woman. It was inexplicable, but it was the way Jessica felt. Karen and Paula both tried to convince Jessica to explore love elsewhere, where it could be reciprocated. The naïvely smitten Jessie was not dissuaded by the advice of her motherly figures, nor was she ever frustrated with Coach's inability to love. She adored Coach for the organism he was.

This eight-year span was devoid of turquoise and green, Coach-like, incidents. His body regularly progressed, like a typical human. The year had just turned over to 2008. Coach has existed on the Earth for ten years, his body appeared like that of a twenty-eight-year-old, and his educational intellect superseded that of a fifty-year-old scholar. He sincerely was an enigma. Paula had supplied Coach with all the reading materials she could obtain, on an array of topics. Eight years is a long time, and Paula kept Coach occupied through most of it with an abundance of literature.

Frank would sporadically check in on the Maker duo, a handful of times per year. Paula appreciated his compassionate heart, his generous personality, and his muscular figure. She had felt attraction towards him in the last two years of checkups when he came around more frequently. Karen would stop by twice a month, more so on Paula's behalf, to catch up and drink wine. She eventually divulged her true profession to Paula on one particularly drunken evening. Karen had changed her role in the CIA to an ancillary, humanitarian department. She was fundamental in the advancement of more compassionate ways of acquiring critical intelligence. Coach's impression on Karen rerouted her life's trajectory, and she was forever grateful. Patricia Plankton, Coach's sixth-grade teacher for two months, visited Paula and Coach once a year for the first four years. But she eventually became the principal at the school and was devoted to molding the future generations of adults. This was Coach's small, but pungent, network of folks that Paula considered as extended family.

The news inside Coach's abbreviated sphere of friends was primarily optimistic. Inversely, the news throughout the world had increasingly grown pessimistic. Over 65 percent of the Earth's wildlife had been ravaged and commercialized by massive, international conglomerates. The greed of mankind dominated the world order. Natural resources were supplanted with poisonous materials. Forests and ecosystems were demolished to proliferate cows and cash crops. The intensity and frequency of natural disasters amplified, and millions of people were displaced from their native land. The global temperature had reached devastatingly new highs. The equilibrium of Earth's natural environment had skewed in irrevocable ways.

Paula would try not to fill Coach's head with these dreadful news summaries, but he would always know when the declarations were on the destruction of Mother Nature. The only time Paula ever saw Coach's smile diminish was when they would watch these ecologically disastrous reports. The Earth had now past its pivotal point of no return. Paula was severely wrong about the depths of human ignorance. She had passionately believed, eight years ago, that the internet and technological advancements would be the human race's redeemer. Social media, and the vast accessibility of information, had adversely impacted the human condition. People did not concern themselves with Earthly dilemmas. Their concerns were dictated by their own manifested narcissism. Humans foolishly entrusted the corrupted authoritative personnel, that reigned over these conglomerates, to 'do the right thing'. The right thing had not been done, and humanity was now confronting its imminent ruin.

Chapter 21:

On February 1st, 2008, Coach had been awakened by an intimately intuitive force. The sheltered young man had left his home, by himself, for the first time in eight years. His feet were bare, and he was wearing only pajama bottoms. The night was hotter than any Tennessee winter night he had experienced, the globe was undoubtedly warming. Coach's walk was steady, and Mother-Naturally guided. He had been robustly strolling for twenty-three minutes when he ascended the Fasser porch. It was 4:12 am when Coach commenced his insistent ringing of the doorbell. Sofia answered the door sleepy-eyed and shocked to see Coach standing there.

"Hola, Senor Coach. What do you need?" Sofia had become fluent in English.

Coach rang the doorbell so stubbornly that both Karen and Victor woke from their slumbers and started down the steps.

"Coach! Are you alright, Sweetie?" Karen asked out of incredulity, knowing she would receive no verbal answer.

"Who the hell is that at this hour!? Victor interjected. He had just been sent home last night due to the critical conditions of the Earth's atmosphere.

Most of the existing CIA missions had been terminated. The organization allowed abidingly estranged, highly ranked, agents, to go home and spend time with their loved ones. Victor Fasser is the Deputy Director of the Central Intelligence Agency; his position requires him to be active and available 24/7. Victor has only been home two other times in the ten years Coach has been alive, for short-term intervals. Mr. Fasser took great pride in his role and performed it with dignity. Victor did not process his sacrifices and atrocious determinations sorrowfully, that is not what Coach came here for. Coach had not provided his grief-sucking-service on anyone in over eight years, he was not here to purge...

"What are you here for?!" Victor demanded an answer from the shirtless man standing on his porch.

"Vick, this is Coach. The one Jess and I have told you about countless times, ease up." Karen refreshed Victor's memory. This was the first time that Coach and victor have met.

Victor's intensely furrowed brow lightened when Karen updated him, "Ahh, yes. The famous Coach! I did not expect to meet you at such an ungodly hour, but it certainly is a pleasure!" he proclaimed with a smile as he held out his hand for a salutation.

"He does not function like the rest of us, Vick. He means no disrespect." Karen quelled the situation as Victor's face read of offense by Coach's physical inaction and boisterous smile.

Jessica was in her second year of college at the local university. She had been living there for most of the year but took trips back home, as often as she could, to see Coach. Jessica pursued a degree in environmental science, hoping to be a part of the shift towards environmental homeostasis. She already planned to make the trip home for the weekend, to visit with her distant father, once she received the news of his return. But it was not even 4:30 am yet. The Fasser's put a sweater on Coach, and Sofia and Karen drove him back home. The front door was still ajar at the Maker household, and Paula was soundly asleep. Sofia shepherded Coach back to his bed, and Karen woke up Paula to inform her of what just transpired.

Karen gently shrugged Paula's shoulder, "Paula, Sweetie. It's Karen. I hate to wake you, but Coach wound up at our doorstep."

Paula slowly opened her left eye, and then the right, before registering what she thought she heard Karen say, "What, you found him where?!" Both eyes were now opened when she finished the question.

"He must have wandered his way to our place, in the night. I'm not sure otherwise." Karen replied honestly and tenderly rubbed Paula's shoulder before continuing, "But it's okay. We got him back safe in his bed."

Paula sat up straight with a dazed and confused expression on her face, adding, "He hasn't done anything like this in eight years or so. There has to be a reason..."

Karen remained with Paula for the morning, as did Sofia, and they discussed potential reasons why Coach would have made a move like this. They huddled around the table and sipped coffee at 5:48 am. Paula insisted that she turn on the news because of the developing stories of rampant wildfires. Natural disasters, like these, were strengthening and destroying much of the Earth's residual flora and fauna. These mortally induced calamities are products of Earth's human virus. We coexist with each other and are meant to with Mother Nature...

"Somewhere along the way, we forgot what mutually beneficially meant." Karen morosely whispered as the report unfolded layers of horrific information.

The television speakers projected, "There are now enormous wildfires simultaneously occurring on six continents across the globe. Scientists are reporting that the persisting fires will increase the levels of carbon dioxide by eighteen percent... And with the excessive deforestation that has materialized over the last five years... There is not enough remaining foliage to absorb the exponential rise of this greenhouse gas. This could leave our planet..."

"Fucked," Paula finished the statement for the reporter.

Paula noticed Coach had been watching from behind the sofa with a frown on his face. He was pointing at the television screen, attempting to communicate in the only way he could. Paula had tried copious times, over

the last eight years, to have Coach communicate through text. It simply was

not a facet of Coach's talents. But his penmanship was flawless during his

studies. This was just another example of the mystifying ways of Coach.

"I know, Honey. It is disheartening to watch the apocalypse happen

in front of your eyes. It's a helpless feeling." Paula sympathetically

acknowledged Coach's discontent.

Coach held his pout, and his finger pointed firmly at the screen. He

did not deviate an inch. "Let's just turn this mess off for now," Paula

suggested while she swiftly pressed the power button on the remote.

The rest of the day had a daunting aura that suffocated its promise of

hope. All the ladies sat in silence after receiving the cataclysmic data, they

finished their coffee and grimly parted ways. Coach's smile returned to his

face after Paula shut off the TV. Momma Maker thought it best they play

the ignorant card and proceed with their educational routine as usual. There

was nothing either of them could do, or perhaps there was solely nothing

that Paula could. Paula did her best to remain passionate during today's lesson, but she was distraught by the magnitude of the worldwide predicament.

Merely forty-five minutes into the lesson, and Coach had gotten up several times to make a break for the exit.

Paula had reeled him in for a third time, declaring, "Coach! Where the hell do you keep trying to go!?" she sat next to him after settling his restless body.

"What the hell is the point, anyway? We are all doomed!" Paula's face collapsed in her hands, and she violently wailed.

While Paula was distracted, wallowing in trepidation, Coach escaped through the front door. Only this time, Coach consciously trotted his way to the Fasser family's porch again. Paula had been parked across the street from the house by the time Coach showed, assuming that this is where he would end up.

"Why, Coach!?" Paula shouted towards Coach as she climbed the porch stairs.

Coach resumed his ruthless ringing of the doorbell. Paula finally made it to Coach's side and snatched his poking member to cease this parade.

Karen answered the door. "I am so sorry for the disturbance, Karen. But our Coach was determined to get back here." Paula apologized as she struggled to maneuver Coach's broad body from the veranda.

"Coach!!" Jessica shouted from inside the house. She ran through the entrance to squeeze her pal. "There is no reason to go to class if the world is ending, eh, Coach!?" Jessie tried to make the statement sound amusing. She, and the rest of the world, had heard the fateful news this dawn.

Karen hauled Paula and Coach into her home, Sofia was preparing breakfast, and Victor was upstairs on the phone. The time was 7:38 am, and the global news was streaming on the Fasser's living room television. The content of the reports had gotten no more encouraging. The recordings showed unrest across the world. Video footage of rainforests engulfed in immense flames stole the show. But there were interludes of humans looting, scurrying, and brawling for resources.

Victor came down the steps with an ominous glare in his eyes, "Hey, it's Coach again!" he tried to diverge everyone's attention from his disturbed face.

As Victor made it to the main floor, he drifted right towards Paula, "Hello there, I don't think we have met. I am Victor Fasser, Jessica's father." He coerced a smile, but his eyes screeched of pure terror.

"It is a pleasure to meet you finally. I am Paula, Coach's mother. You certainly are a busy man, Mr. Fasser." Paula responded as jubilant as she could muster. It was all a façade. They both knew of the planet's impending doom. Victor's eyes led on that he probably knew more specifics about this misfortune.

Chapter 22:

Paula and Coach were invited to have breakfast with the Fasser family. The table supported a delightful exhibit of scrambled eggs, waffles, bacon, fruit salad and toasts. But no one seemed to have much of an appetite this morning, except Coach. He wolfed down his mixture of everything but bacon. It was entertaining to watch Coach smile and devour his breakfast as if it were just any other day. The rest of the crew at the table swigged coffee and alternatively chuckled at Coach's syrup-drenched smile. It was refreshing for everyone to laugh. They did not want that feeling to fade.

The laughing sustained as Coach continued gorging. After ten seconds, Victor's laugh sounded different. The cadence had altered. His chuckle had turned into a cry.

Karen, who was sitting next to Victor, put her arm around him and summoned, "Babe, what's wrong? Who was that on the phone?"

Victor looked up at the two unfamiliar faces and refused to confess any classified information in front of them. He could not help it. Victor's entire life had been built around confidentiality.

"It's okay, Vick. They are family. You can speak freely around Coach and Paula." Karen did her best to guarantee him.

Victor peered around the table, still contemplating his verdict on whether he should disclose. He then spouted, "What the fuck difference does it make? We will all be dead soon enough."

Sofia gasped after hearing what Mr. Fasser had said. She had never heard him speak such despondent language.

"That was the White House Chief of Staff. He said that the information they received is dire..." Victor took a sip of coffee to clear his throat "... They have scientific data revealing that these fires will consequently cause an unsustainable atmosphere in a matter of months."

"How many months, Vick?!" Karen urged Victor to unveil the entire truth.

Victor had tears flowing down his face again when he replied, "Less than two."

The sad breakfast club chewed on that harshly realistic timeframe for a few minutes of silence. Paula broke the silence by posing a string of questions. Karen had disclosed to her that Victor "worked for the government." But she had no idea he was such a prominent figure, like the Deputy Director of the CIA. Jessica had finally been told the truth about her father while she was in high school, so she had known for a few years. Paula, Karen, and Jessica all attacked Victor with questions about his career. They inquired about the phone call he received, the devastating timeline, and any potential resolutions.

"They explicitly said there is nothing they can do! No way to cultivate sufficient plant life, and at a fast-enough rate, to absorb this much carbon dioxide!" Victor gave his clearest effort at elaboration.

As soon as Victor finished his statement, Paula, and Jessica locked eyes. Both ladies were thinking of the same answer, Coach. It struck Paula like a bolt of lightning. This was Coach's destiny, Jessie realized it too. Karen had not witnessed Coach's extraordinarily botanical purging, but she experienced his exorcising capabilities. Each entity at the table took turns glancing at Coach's wide grin. Victor was perplexed, and he made sure everyone knew it. Karen and Jessica reiterated that they had explained some of these occurrences to him before.

"I thought you gals were spinning some supernatural stories up!" Victor skeptically stated.

They continued their caucus at the table. Each person was brought up to speed, and all the information about Coach was exchanged. From the homeless man in the park to Greg's unfortunate death, all the substance was laid out.

"I believe what you all are telling me, but I have been told wilder fables in my day." Victor candidly acknowledged after hearing the whole story. He was not convinced.

Jessica glowered at her father's cynicism, and requested, "Then get us two or three of the saddest people you know, individuals that are inconsolable. Coach will show you himself!"

"... But it seems to be specifically people suffering from the loss of others close to them. Immediate family members, friends and such." Paula specified, recalling from her recorded observations.

"Done and done. I know plenty. You need two or three?" Victor responded unsympathetically; his line of work left a lot of families fractured.

"Two should be fine," answered Paula. She remembered from her journal that Coach's botanical purging typically happens after about three of his turquoise exorcisms. And he still had the old man from the crematorium's anguish in him somewhere. Paula was relying on the

resiliency of Coach's anomalies. Paula figured that the sorrow Coach has

absorbed, years ago, does not have an expiration date.

"I'm on it!" Victor sprang into action. He thought to himself, "What

do we all have to lose, anyway? At least this ridiculous endeavor will keep

our minds occupied." Victor needed to see it to believe it.

Victor made bids to some of his recently fallen comrades' widows.

He tried his best not to sound crazy on the phone while he explained parts

of Coach's tale. The ladies at the Fasser's table resumed swapping Coach-

related stories. They shared theories and intel, all while Coach sat at the

table and smiled. Coach's smile appeared different to Paula in this moment.

It exuded a distinct air as if he were smiling at them all piecing the puzzle

together, satisfied in seeing the mystery being solved.

"After Roger dropped Coach off, and he worked his magic on Greg

and me. I recall Roger saying that he had Coach for over a year after his

enlightenment." Paula was utilizing all the previous histories of Coach she

could drudge up. She was attempting to illustrate a parallel between

Coach's recently latent duration of time and his inevitably vegetal expulsion.

"If he held it for over a year before, with Roger... What is seven more, eh, Coach?" Paula facetiously commented on Coach's retention of people's anguish. Although the ladies at the table were successfully clarifying their timelines and correlations about Coach, not every dot connected. Not every dot would connect. Paula's relationship with Coach has been substantial, but it has also been relatively short.

"It is the way it's supposed to be." Paula believed this statement as she repeated it in her head. They must clutch to the hope they have left about hypothetically restoring the Earth.

Chapter 23:

The afternoon was slipping away. It was now 3:41 pm. Victor had convinced two grieving widows to come join them for dinner. The first one is Christine Plumm, she lost her husband one year ago, and her parents when she was a little girl. Christine lives two hours north of the Fasser household, and she agreed to arrive at four pm promptly. The second widow is Hillary Wells. She lost her husband three years ago. Just this past year,

Hillary lost her son to Leukemia. Hillary had not left the house much since her son's death, but she agreed to take the hour-long drive for the promise of potential relief.

The clock struck 3:59 pm, and the punctual women were both standing on the Fasser family's porch. They were military wives, so they had adjusted to the timely lifestyle. Christine and Hillary were chatting on the porch, validating the fantastical story that Victor had told each of them. Coach's senses were tingling. He stood up from his seat on the couch while Victor opened the door. The guests pleasantly greeted Victor, and he steered them into the home.

"Vick, I appreciate the call earlier. But that was one hell of a story you tried sellin' me on the phone." Christine uttered, and then snickered after she finished hugging Karen.

Hillary softly said, "Hello, everybody." Her tone resonated with melancholy, and her demeanor was constricted.

"Take a seat on the sofa there, ladies." Victor ushered them to the open spots.

Jessica was holding back Coach the best she could. She could hardly contain the force of his physical drive.

"Somebody has got to expla-" before Christine could finish, Coach broke free from Jessie's barrier and gravitated to the seated women.

The two bereaved individuals were sitting together on the sofa. Coach had a hand on each. He was standing behind the couch, and his skin was gleaming its patented turquoise tinge. Victor's eyes were fixated on the spectacle in his living room. The moans and groans that came from the women were disturbingly charming, such pain and relief combined into one extraordinary affair. The convergence lasted just over a minute before the women reverted to reality with smirks of glee. Coach collapsed to the floor behind them, and Paula and Jessica ran to his aide.

Victor snapped out of his shocked state to ask the women, "How do you ladies feel?"

The tsunami of elation that came from these women was overwhelmingly wonderful. Hillary's posture had rectified, and her voice was bright. Christine thanked and hugged every person in the room, affirming that she has never felt better in her life.

"It's just too bad the world is ending... I would have liked to keep on feelin' this way." Christine charmingly remarked on humanity's terrifying destiny.

"I don't know what that was, but it feels like my heart can breathe again," Hillary stated in concurrence with Christine's sentiments.

Victor was stunned by this mysterious transformation. He reiterated his offer for them to stay for supper. The eased ladies both agreed, they wanted to know more about what just happened. Victor moved Coach's dormant body to the sofa, and Sofia prepared an assortment of empanadas for dinner. The gang of Coach's disciples feasted, exchanged anecdotes, and momentarily distracted themselves from their dystopian future. The dinner concluded with Hillary and Christine's excessively thankful departure from all of Coach's supporters. Before exiting the home, they each gave Coach a loving peck on the forehead.

"That boy is something special. If he had more time, he could have changed the world." Christine signed off with this suitable announcement, unaware of their intentions for Coach.

Hillary smiled and slightly bowed out of graciousness. When she left, she simply said, "You are all so wonderful. Please, do thank him for me."

The transferences were accomplished. Coach was conked out like he always was after doing his thing. It was just a matter of time now.

Victor closed the door behind the discharged women and immediately turned to address the remaining patrons. "That was remarkable! There is no doubt about it. But I am not sure how that is going to save the environment?" Victor confusingly professed.

"Just have to be patient," Paula implored Victor as he continued pressing for answers.

The night grew long, and all of Coach's friends and family nodded off in the living room, except for Jessie. She had been sitting at the end of the sofa under Coach's bare feet, confident that he was their savior. Jessica needed to make sure she was alert to notify the others when the time comes. Coach always left his feet bare, never had Jessica recalled seeing him in socks.

The time was 1:54 am when Jessie felt Coach rumbling awake.
"Guys, it's showtime," Jessie whispered in the muted living room. There
was only the soft glow of the television perpetually running disastrous news
updates. Coach had made it to the door before Jessica could rouse the
adults. The rest of them sluggishly arose to see the front door agape, Coach
was on the move. Paula suggested they take Victor's large, Yukon SUV, for
the extra cargo on the ride back. Team Coach piled into the spacious vehicle
and trailed the terrestrial being while he paced barefoot through the desolate
street.

Roughly two miles north of the Fasser dwelling was an abandoned
warehouse, where industrial cleaning products were once produced and
stored. This nasty place was shut down by the state due to the particularly
excessive number of cancer-related deaths throughout the warehouse staff.
These synthetically derived, venomous, molecules ultimately leeched into
the grounds surrounding the depot. This was Paula's best guess as to where
Coach was heading, and she was correct.

The gang followed Coach for thirty minutes, until he reached the
fenced perimeter of this waste site. Without hesitation, Coach scaled the

ten-foot chain-linked fence to get his feet on the tainted ground. The group

of followers dismounted from the Yukon and Coach was already twenty

yards into the hazardous land. Coach's body was contorting into the

hunched position while the fire in his feet made him feel powerfully

nauseated. This land was poisoned to an excessive degree. It would not take

Coach long to release life unto this spoiled estate. Thirty-five yards in and

Coach had launched the liberation of his numinously turquoise sludge.

Jessica glanced over to make sure that her father was paying

attention to the revoltingly brilliant vomiting. Victor had not veered his

gaze one time since he had gotten out of the car. Coach projected his radiant

refuse in a customarily sporadic manner across this noxious land. It was the

most toxic Earth he had yet to encounter. Coach's instinct was to spray as

much area as he could encompass. The night was dangerously warm for

February, and land such as this seemed ubiquitous throughout the world. It

was another sign of human disregard for nature's welfare.

Coach had ousted the spore-riddled slurry for over a minute,

covering up to 30 yards in front of him. He buckled after he was emptied,

and the instantaneous emergence of enchanting life ensued. Within two minutes of awestruck screening, Victor, Karen, Paula, Jessica, and Sofia had witnessed the formulation of a complex patch of forestry.

"What do you think now, Dad?!" Jessica condescendingly asked her father.

Paula called to Victor from the locked gate, "Hey Vick, do you have any tools in your car that might help us get this entrance open?!"

Victor snapped to and hopped into the driver's seat. He screamed out of the window, "Everyone out of the way!" Vick accelerated through the fastened gate with no concern for his automobile's front end. He was now a believer.

The rest of the group ran through the entryway, and into the brush, in search of Coach. Victor confiscated a variety of foliage from the perimeter of the forest and compiled it in a duffle bag he had in the trunk of his car. Victor knew exactly where to bring these samples. Inspiration saturated his hitherto dreary soul.

"Vick! Come help us!" Karen called to Victor from some indiscernible position inside a wall of ferally giant grasses.

Victor roamed around for a few minutes, lost in wonder, passively searching for Coach and the ladies. By the time he had found the impressed moss patch where Coach was lain, the ladies had carried Coach back to the car.

Victor was standing in awe at the inexplicable sight of sudden plant life. His eyes welled while he whispered to himself, "This could be the answer. Coach is our salvation." He smiled as the feelings of despair temporarily faded.

Everyone returned to the Yukon, and Victor sped the entire ride home. He was determined to get Coach's botanical samples to the Office of Science and Technology. It is an integral research and development department of the Executive Office in the United States federal government. Victor was certain that they would have the equipment and technology to derive a serum or solution to the crisis. As soon as they all returned to the Fasser house, they got Coach settled inside, and Victor ran upstairs to start his assault of calls.

"That was unbelievable!" Karen professed after recollecting her thoughts.

"... And tomorrow, Coach will look like a thirty-year-old man."
Paula candidly expressed to the rest of the crew.

Jessica and Paula passionately swapped interpretations of tonight's
adventure while Coach rested on the sofa next to them. Karen had stepped
away to settle her befuddled mind, and Sofia stayed occupied in the kitchen.

A few minutes passed by before Victor rushed downstairs,
proclaiming, "I am headed to D.C right now! I have to get these samples of
plant life to the Science and Technology Department, ASAP!" Vick kissed
everyone goodbye and scurried to a private jet awaiting him at the local
airport.

"This is exciting! There could be some magical answer to our
prayers in the exotic foliage Coach just created." Karen optimistically
stated.

The rest of the early morning consisted of speculations about Coach
and the anticipated results that Victor absconded to procure.

"Did you notice the way Coach was walking across the ground
before he spewed everywhere?" Jessica mentioned her observation. "His

irregular steps made it seem like he was in pain." She continued her conjecture.

"I did notice. Perhaps, that is where Coach becomes the conduit between death and life." Paula reflexively answered Jessie's question with an uncanny premise.

"Wow, Paula! That could be it! I have never thought about it in that manner. And I have spent A LOT of time thinking about this!" Jessica was excited about the progressive elucidations they were making on behalf of Coach's mysterious existence.

"It's like he draws the pain from the Earth, and it coalesces with the pain he sources from humans. He somehow internally converts this combined pain into some wildly effective natural concoction..." Jessie was on a roll after Paula bridged a critical gap in her theories.

"... Then, he emits the turquoise mess to bring new life to a place submerged in death." Paula finished Jessica's train of thought.

The rest of this February 2nd consisted of stimulating talks about Coach's journey. The journey that led him to Greg and Paula. The same journey that guided him to Jessica's life and that kept him safe until the brink of the human species' extinction. Jessica and Paula were utterly persuaded that he was of a divine breed.

Chapter 24:

Coach arose from the Fasser's sofa around 7:15 pm. The women in the house were finishing a late dinner at the table. Karen, Paula, Jessie, and Sofia all turned their heads to gawk at the strangely aged Coach. His garments had slackened, his skin was noticeably rougher, and his face was thickly bearded. Paula had been meticulous about manicuring Coach's hair during the predominantly isolated, eight-year stint. But it had grown numerous inches during his latest time-out. Coach had intermittent grey hairs in his mane. Coach looked like he was older than thirty; he looked more like a man closer to his mid-forties, already past his half-life.

"Good Lord, Coach!" Paula exclaimed as she shot up from her chair. "You look like you've aged fifteen years!" she was too shocked to hold her bewilderment inside.

This disproportionate aging of Coach was contradictory to Paula's records. But the last nine years of her life were disproportionate to everything she thought she understood. Before she got worked up, Paula

repeated to herself, "It is the way it's supposed to be."

Victor called Karen's cellphone, Paula and Jessica watched her

expressions dramatically shift as she received unsavory information. Karen

tossed her phone down on the table and sunk into the nearest seat.

"What is it, Karen!? What's the word?!" Paula barked at Karen in

this auspicious moment.

"It was a failure. The leaves, or whatever Victor brought them, were

inclusively common." Karen did not lift her brooding head as she answered.

"What else did he say?! That can't be it!" Paula shouted to galvanize

Karen. She was not dissuaded from her certainty of Coach's purpose in this

quandary.

"...They would need the source...To acquire further samples..."

Karen had sobbed while she answered.

They all were reasonably certain as to what that meant. It meant the

eventual termination of Coach. No one said anything else for the next minute. It was an emotional convention for every one of these women that had been touched by Coach in some fruitful way.

"It is the way it's supposed to be." Paula articulated aloud, speaking over the sniffling whines of sadness.

This was Paula's affirmation to stop impeding Coach from doing what he did. Coach smiled back at all the somber faces glaring at him with worry. His timeless smile was unintentionally communicating to them that, "it is going to be alright." Karen called Victor back and relayed the message to get Coach. Mr. Fasser informed the scientists, near Washington D.C., of his immediate return with the subject. He vigorously encouraged them to prepare any, and all, of the requisite components for experimentation and synthesis. Time is of the essence.

Paula decided that it would be far too grueling for her to watch what would happen to her precious Coach. Coach's confidant, Jessica, agreed to accompany him to his journey's end. Karen and Sofia would remain back at home with Paula, but first, they all said their farewells.

"You are a blessing with a curse, Sweet Coach. Thank you, does not do it justice." Karen kissed Coach's bearded cheek and squeezed him for well over a minute.

Sofia was next to Karen, waiting to embrace Coach. She whispered something endearing in his ear before hugging his stagnantly tall body. All Coach could offer back was a smile.

The ladies switched out positions until it was Paula's turn to meet Coach's grin. Paula's eyes were red from clearing out her tear ducts. Her life had become a turbulent and unique ride since Coach graced her with his extraordinary aura. Momma Maker accepted that her reign of supervision was now over, she knew it was only temporary to begin with. Yet, it did not make this moment any easier for her. Coach had become her life, her reason for living, and her son. The Earth needs Coach though. Paula's heart was aching, but she felt her pride for Coach simmering topmost amongst the flood of emotions.

"You go save the Earth, my Coach," Paula whispered into his mysterious mind during the end of their last embrace. Coach returned his smile. There were no tears like when Roger left him as an adolescent. There was no need to showcase his capabilities any longer.

Jessica led Coach to her car and away from his loved ones. She knew she must be Coach's logistical catalyst, and confidant, in this next chapter of his expedition. Victor wasted no time returning the jet plane to Tennessee to obtain Coach. By the time Jessie and Coach reached the runway, the jet was already in position for their boarding. Coach had never been on a plane before. There was plenty Coach has never done. There was plenty he would never do.

The aircraft landed in Washington, D.C., where a black SUV awaited Coach and the Fasser party. The global news reported of the escalating fires but did not disclose the catastrophic timeline. It was doubtful that the media was entirely abreast of the rapidly looming obliteration of mankind. The government keeps this dystopian information from the masses if they can. Victor knew, though, and he zipped along as if the timeline had hastened.

The black SUV rushed Coach, Jessica, and Victor to an isolated warehouse in Maryland. This lot of land inhabited government-funded, clandestine, research and development. A concealed elevator in the lobby brought the trio down several stories. The fortify elevator doors split open to a vast scientific hub that had white lab coats buzzing about. There was debating and vindicating swirling through this underground cavity's ether. Victor had his hand clenched on Coach's arm the entire ride down. He maneuvered Coach to his corresponding laboratory.

"You stay here, Honey." Victor pointed to a breakroom on the way to the test center.

"... You're not going to want to see this part." Victor mumbled to himself, and Coach, as Jessica remained reluctantly static behind them.

Chapter 25:

The towering, chrome, door opened automatically, and one of the scientist's locked it behind Coach and Victor. There was a vertically supported stretcher equipped with several sections of harnesses. The lead doctor's name was Raymond Klint. He was assisted by two other researchers that specialized in ecology. Dr. Klint ordered one specialist to strap the subject into the stretcher. Coach was restricted and smiling when the prodding began. They started by drawing blood from every limb on Coach's body.

Dr. Klint commented as he extracted Coach's juices from his arm, "... Fascinating, the color is atypical. The fluid seems to be composed of a higher viscosity than human blood... "

All three of the scientists operated in unison. It was like a well-choreographed ballet.

"Now, the saliva samples." Dr. Klint ordered, and one scientist swabbed the inside of Coach's smiling mouth.

Dr. Klint was an ornery old physician. His career for the government had turned him jaded and abrasive in his methods. Coach tried his hardest to reach for the sad, venerable man as the sampling continued. They tore several of Coach's fingernails out and Dr. Klint cut out portions of Coach's flesh. They removed hair from several areas of his body, and one of the scientist's unsympathetically plucked multiple teeth from Coach's mouth. Turquoise blood was slowly streaming from Coach's cheerful lips. As one of the scientist's reached to gather a sample from Coach's oozing orifice, the skin on his wrist was exposed. Coach inadvertently coughed on the slim portion of exposed skin. Only a few drops had landed. But it was enough.

"My God, it burns!" the man shrieked as his skin bubbled in front of his own eyes. The turquoise sprinkles turned brown as they melted through tissue and cartilage.

"... Interesting," Dr. Klint callously remarked from the other side of Coach.

The man was shrieking in agony as four molten holes tunneled through his wrist, rendering him unconscious.

"Someone clean up this mess! And send in another assistant!" Dr. Klint shouted orders as he scrupulously filleted Coach's membrane.

The fresh assistant entered the room as two auxiliary workers carried away the comatose amputee. Dr. Klint stuck a wondrously thin needle into Coach's left eye to extract its unusual liquids.

Victor, who was hideously watching from afar, shouted, "Is that necessary?!" referring to the penetration of Coach's cornea.

"We are trying to save the planet, yes? Let me do my job then!" Dr. K cruelly responded to Victor. The doctor was aiming to collect all the samples that Coach's vessel offered. Coach's smile never faded through the whole process. Not a peep was made. Not even so much as a wince.

"The magic happens in his vomit!" Victor shouted before Dr. Klint could jam any more needles into Coach.

"Scalpel!" Raymond Klint directed one assistant to load his hand with the razor-sharp cutting apparatus.

As Dr. Klint coldheartedly began to slice through Coach's abdomen vertically, Victor hollered, "Stop!" the doctor had almost reached Coach's belly button before Victor continued, "There is a more humane way!"

"Deputy Fasser! I was under the impression that time was of the essence. And I was to do any, and all, vital analyses on this subject." Dr. Klint scornfully responded. He had removed the scalpel from Coach's exposed midsection; turquoise blood gurgled and poured from the bizarrely colored cavity.

"Just release one of his arms, you heartless bastard!" Victor ordered the curmudgeonly old man, as his superior.

Raymond Klint cautiously unbound Coach's stained left arm. As soon as it was free, and before Dr. Klint could make another sly remark to Victor, Coach had attached his unrestricted limb to the doctor. The turquoise show began, and Raymond's past year of concentrated sorrow washed away. Klint's anguish about his recently departed wife of forty-three years was removed from his dampened sixty-eight-year-old soul. The process took just over a minute and Coach fainted in his secured carriage, afterwards.

Dr. Klint collected himself up from the ground and regained his balanced before pontificating, "This being is a cherub! I thought I would certainly go to my grave with the pain of losing Eveline, after forty-three years." Raymond's cantankerous appearance renovated into a delighted state.

The assistants were in awe at the gruesome and glorious scene they were witnesses to, "Do me next!" one of them yelled.

"It doesn't work like that, Kid." Victor assured both of the young assistants, and added, "It has to be grief brought on by the loss of a dear loved one."

"We know plenty of people working here who have lost a mother or someone important to them." The other assistant announced to help the cause.

"Go round-up as many as you can, boys!" Victor hearteningly replied to the young man's suggestion.

"What do we do about him?" Dr. Klint inquired towards Coach's flaccid and leaking body.

"You can start by patching the poor sonofabitch up," Victor sneeringly replied, insinuating toward the hole in Coach's upper body. "Then, gather all the epinephrine you have on this base." Victor's wheels were spinning now. He knew this would still likely destroy Coach. But Vick could not stand to see Coach dissected. Not after viewing all the affection that his family had for him.

There was now a line of solemn scientists stretching through the laboratory doorway. Dr. Klint had mended Coach's lacerations while he was still resting. Jessica was anxiously pacing within the break room, twenty yards from the test center. Coach was fastened in the heart of this bleak and expansive workroom.

Dr. Klint injected Coach with adrenaline to bring him back for the next wave of experimentation. Coach's eyes rushed open as the epinephrine rapidly coursed through his veins. The first worker in line stepped up to Coach, as instructed. The man's cat recently died. It was not enough to entice Coach's aptitude.

Victor screamed out, "Next!"

The second contestant made his way up to Coach. His girlfriend recently broke up with him. He put his palm on Coach, but nothing turquoise would occur.

"Next!" Victor shouted impatiently. "Hey, you! I thought you said you knew guys with real suffering?!" Vick directed his probe at one assistant.

Upon completion of Victor's complaint, the third participant struck turquoise. Coach contacted him as soon as he was close enough. The illumination provoked the rest of the contributors in line, two immediately stepped away. This one that Coach was locked onto had just lost his mother last month. The young man steadily produced sounds that he has never made before. Coach passed out again after the transference was achieved.

"Holy shit! I feel free!" the young man hollered at the remaining line of employees, and he stormed off into the lobby of this covert hub.

The next eighteen minutes consisted of Coach being pumped full of adrenaline, sorting through the fallaciously mournful, and Coach passing back out after a successful connection. Rinse and repeat. Or rather, inject and repeat. Every second cycle, Coach's hair would get a little longer, his skin a little drier, and his eyes a little wearier. Coach did not get his normally allotted time to recover between exorcisms. He was erratically maturing. Coach's heart was weakening with every syringe full of epinephrine, and his organs were all ripening. Victor and Dr. Klint kept the vicious cycle continuing as they repeatedly sent over participants, as soon as Coach was conscious again. They must have pushed through sixteen people, six of which there were successful conveyances.

"This young man's heart is not sounding too staunch anymore." The doctor reported after examining Coach's pulse with his stethoscope. "His physical body is deteriorating as well. I have never seen anything like it," Raymond Klint added out of medicinal astonishment.

"This is magnificent and all... But what is the next phase?" Dr. Klint doubted Victor's bid for this alternative plan. "I do not want to revert to the original strategy, but it may be our last chance." Raymond was referring to disemboweling Coach. Klint resumed speaking while Victor pondered on what to do next.

"I am not sure what the problem is. I have seen Coach purge gallons of this turquoise muck myself. It happened just the other day... " Victor continued speculating with the information he had "... Coach's mother added that he routinely purges after he does the turquoise thing on at least three people."

"We are at six individuals now!" one of the assistant's interjected from behind Victor.

"Yes. I am aware of this, Kid. I have been here the whole time!" Victor was in no mood for the stating of the obvious. "Give me a minute. Don't you dare gut this man!" Victor instructed Dr. Klint to stand down on his reversion of their plan, and he sprinted to go retrieve his daughter.

Chapter 26:

Jessica had been waiting as patiently as she could in the breakroom. Her mind was racing from the worries she felt in this place and on this Earth. Victor hustled around the corner to discover Jessie sitting at the dining table. She had her head down on the backs of her hands.

Jessie shot up when she heard the door creak, "Dad?! What is going on?" she asked her father, who was breathing heavily from all the exertion.

Victor filled his daughter in on the predicament, leaving out some of the gorier details about Coach's voluntary torment. "We have done the turquoise thing on six people now, but he has yet to do the vomit thing. I don't know what I am doing here, Jess!" Victor was frantic in his response.

"From what I have observed, Coach has always been drawn to polluted land before he hurled," Jessica replied to her father and stood up from her seat. "I want to see Coach right now!" she demanded, concerned about the state of her best friend.

Victor escorted his daughter to Coach who appeared as a disheveled mess in the capacious laboratory. Coach was coated with bloodied bandages all across his limbs. His torso was wrapped in gauze, saturated with the blueish-green liquid. Coach had one eye closed where a trail of pale fluid ran from. His smile displayed missing teeth. Coach's chin and neck were encased with more turquoise. Coach's clothing had been removed, except for his boxer-briefs, they had not made it to his genitalia. Jessie noticed Coach's gradually wrinkling skin. Her friend had silver-saturated and untamed locks accompanied with a shaggily pepper-colored beard. Coach looked like a prisoner of war that had returned home after years of torture. He looked like a decrypt old man.

Jessica was sobbing after examining her brutalized friend, "What the hell did you do to him?!" Coach was awoken just before Jessica entered the lab, and he held his smile true.

"Everybody out!" Victor shouted at the remaining few candidates for the Coach experience.

It was just Coach, Dr. Klint, Victor and one assistant left in the workshop. The other assistant had been instructed to get a wheelchair. Victor explained the arduous features of this ordeal to Jessica, hoping that she could enlighten them. Jessica draped Coach in the nearest lab coat she could get her hands on.

"Honey, we had to be cruel in this instance. I would have sacrificed my flesh and blood if it meant saving the world." Victor tried to console his agitated offspring.

Coach was still steadily wilting away as the minutes lapsed. His body was processing the onslaught of six exorcisms and over four milligrams of epinephrine, in less than an hour. It was now a race against Coach's biological clock and the Earth's. The smiling Coach was liberated from the gurney and assisted into a wheelchair.

"The others have been running the tests on Coach's DNA samples we removed... " Before Dr. Klint finished his statement, he peered over at a seething Jessica standing behind Coach's wheelchair. "... Coach only has small traces of human genetics. His DNA is unidentifiable, but it certainly is not purely of the human species."

"I could have told you that, Doc! And I have only known him for a couple of days. What does that mean for the redemption of the Earth?!" Victor implored Dr. Klint to give him something encouraging.

He had nothing to offer, lamentably answering, "It does not mean anything, unfortunately. Those samples exhibited no signs of accelerated growth or molecular mutation. They are just enigmatic."

"What do we do next, Klint?! I'm the CIA guy. This science shit is your bag!" Victor grew restless, feverishly pacing back and forth in the lab.

"Victor calm down. We have a little bit of time left to figure this out," Dr. Klint replied with the most comforting reaction he could.

Vick stopped in his tracks and shouted back, "No, we don't! You dumb sonofabitch! They told me we have eleven days. This was our last chance!"

Victor had forgotten his beloved daughter was standing in the room with them. Vick felt a salty liquid morsel trickle down his cheek. He was picturing Jessica burning in the infernos swallowing the rest of Earth's natural landscape. Victor would do whatever he can, while he is still breathing, to avoid that culmination.

"What about Coach's insides? Did you end up gathering any of those samples?!" Victor vehemently stressed his inquisition on Dr. Klint. He knew Jessica would not like the circumstances of this conversation.

"No, we did not actually, just Coach's blood. You requested I free his hand, and he delivered his magic on me before I could. Do you recall?" Raymond refreshed Victor's memory about the very recent past, and they both contributed towards a mutual understanding.

"Gut him." Victor proclaimed. He had abruptly turned ruthless in this desperate situation.

Dr. Klint grabbed the scalpel on the table and the two, deranged with fear, charged towards Coach's jovial and decrypt figure. It was survival time.

"STOOOP!" Jessica screamed as loud as she could, and the sound echoed through the rafters.

Raymond Klint was stunned by the ferocity of her shout. Victor had only been slowed down in his course of action. He instructed, "Get out of the way, Honey. This is our last hope!" Victor was unquenchably determined to get results. He had a scalpel firmly gripped in his hand, inching closer to Coach's seated cadaver.

"All we need to do is find some contaminated soil! There's got to be some around this territory!" Jessie tried to remain calm as her lunatic father swerved around Coach like a shark circling its prey.

"Snap out of it, Vick!" Raymond shuffled over to Victor's mesmerized glare and slapped him across the face.

"This laboratory we are in was formed from tainted soil. If we get to the surface, it shouldn't be far at all until we find some polluted earth." Dr. Klint hustled to the laboratory closet, where he had more sampling containers and equipment.

"May cooler heads prevail. Thanks for being wiser than your old man." Victor hugged his clever daughter and then took control of Coach's wheelchair to speed things along.

Victor seemed back to his normal self, Dr. Klint was almost done gathering adequate supplies, and the lab assistants had cleared a path.

Jessica was proudly standing right beside her confidant through the entire route up to the surface. Coach was lethargically withering away, but his smile was sturdier than ever. His face never articulated feelings of pain, and he had never spoken a word in his lifetime.

"Of course, he is an alien." Jessie declared in the elevator as they lifted several stories back up.

"Not necessarily, young lady. Coach's DNA is fully constructed of Earth-produced, organic matter. It is just not distinguishable with any of our current databases." Dr. Klint clarified on this scientific deposition and Jessica's woes.

"Coach is derived from some biological hybridization. Some form of nature... It was the principal reason I was ready to slice him open after the first go-round." Dr. K said with a calloused chuckle as the elevator doors parted.

Chapter 27:

Victor wheeled Coach through the parking structure and out to the surrounding area. Raymond was right. This was a barren land they were stationed at. They had gotten only ten feet into the deserted terrain before

Coach abruptly bounced out of the wheelchair like a spring chicken. His

walk was steady and concise. Coach's feet felt fiery as he stepped forward.

It was early morning on February 3rd, and the world was hotter still. But the

temperature Coach was feeling came from a different source.

As they watched Coach hobble along, Dr. Klint provided some

context, "There was a ghastly oil spill here before it was deemed

uninhabitable, and then the government claimed the land." Coach locked

into his hunched position.

"You better get your ass over to Coach, Doc. He's going to blow

soon." Victor insisted to Raymond. He pointed at Coach's wrinkly and

awkward posture, ten yards ahead.

Jessica and Victor stayed back and giggled at the doctor's anxious

and perplexed demeanor. Dr. Klint stood to the side of Coach watching and

waiting for something extraordinary. Raymond turned his head back to get

endorsements from either Victor or Jessica about Coach's status. When

Raymond returned his gaze forward, the geyser of turquoise slush came

plummeting from Coach's face. It lasted longer than any other cleansing

Coach had before, it was to be his last purge. Besides, he did just exorcise

six individuals' sorrow, and he was pumped full of a goliath's dose of

adrenaline.

Dr. Klint knelt next to Coach as he released his turquoise fluid.

Raymond collected three-gallon sized containers of the mixture. Typically,

the turquoise base immediately metamorphosized into glorious vegetation

as it inevitably did in this instance. But the restriction of oxygen in the

vacuum-sealed jars kept the turquoise slime samples in liquefied form. The

scientists needed this goopy substance in this precise physical state so that

they can inject it into the synthesis machine. Raymond Klint, and the rest of

his scientific team, had collaborated and prepared while Victor returned to

Tennessee to retrieve Coach. All they needed was the appropriate

ingredient.

The synthesis machine was already queued up for action and

reaction. It was programmed to produce a stable derivative of Coach's

turquoise genius. Victor had so adamantly stressed the importance of one

other specific aspect. The substance must be mass-generated. Time was still of the essence for humankind. The environment would need vast, and expeditious, quantities of this turquoise substance.

Doctor Klint thanked Coach one more time before returning down to his laboratory to continue conducting their reverse-annihilation campaign. The planet's disastrous wildfires were unstoppably raging on throughout its sphere. Victor was told that the anticipated ending juncture for the conflagrations was three days. This was to be the point when the drastic drop in the atmosphere's oxygen levels would be too low to sustain even the wildfires. Then seven grueling days would persist in the painful extinction of all oxygen-breathing organisms. But the projections have just been invalidated, thanks to Coach.

Victor got on the horn and informed all governmental departments of the homo sapiens' inexplicably optimistic turn of fortune. The United States Air Force was mobilized across this scorched Earth for the distribution of Coach's turquoise essence. The lab spent the next forty-eight hours vigorously producing as much of this turquoise solution as their silos could confine. It was a continuous production of metric tons of fluid. The jets would fly into the deserted Maryland territory by twos, land near an isolated patch of mind-bogglingly beautiful forest, and load up with several

tanks of solution. The coordinated procession carried on for the next three

days straight, until there was a foundation established towards

environmental equilibrium.

The plan of action involved revitalizing the lands already

demolished, first. While the Army, Navy, and other international

organizations continued the battle against the residual wildfires. It took five

days of a united, global, and anthropological effort to restore homeostasis

throughout the Earth's environment. The miraculously intense upsurge of

natural growth had cultures from China to Chile unknowingly grateful, to

the American Government. People would never know their true savior. The

real source of their salvation. They would never know about their Coach.

Chapter 28:

Back at the lab's bordering vicinity, on that momentous February

day, Coach was swiftly diminishing in front of Jessica's apprehensive eyes.

Jessie tried her best to contain her dread, and she spoke softly to

Coach, "You did it, My Love. You saved us like I always knew you would." She kissed Coach's wrinkly cheek. Coach lifted his geriatric wing and extended it towards the black SUV in the parking lot.

"You want to go somewhere, Coach?!" Jessica excitedly responded to Coach's movements and looked up at her father to confirm Coach's request.

Dr. Klint verified with Victor, "We have all the trials we need, Vick. Let that poor creature go."

"We can take Coach wherever he wants to go. He's earned as much." Victor promised his daughter after he received the doctor's affirmation of experimental success.

Victor and Jessica cooperatively piled Coach's perishing corpse, and his wheelchair, into the SUV. Victor stayed behind at the facility to maintain the coordinated, Earth-saving efforts. He saluted Coach for all that he has provided the human genus.

"You go ahead without me, Jess. I am going to stay here and make sure things operate smoothly... " Victor finished securing Coach to his seat and hugged his daughter goodbye. "... Carson will drive you to the private jet at the airport. The pilot will take both of you wherever you wish. I made sure of it. I love you both." Victor made his announcements and then closed the passenger door. Jessica swore she heard her father say he loved both of them. She had never heard her father express love for anyone but Karen and her. If there was any other to love, it was surely Coach.

Coach and Jessica were escorted directly to the plane's aperture, and up to the cabin. The Earth was congruently being saved due to Coach's exquisite forces. It was time to save what little life Coach had left. Jessie ran to support Coach's frail body from the car.

"You never stop smiling, Coach! I'll never forget it." Jessica hollered in Coach's crinkled ear as they passed by the rumbling jet engines.

Jessie had Coach's right arm wrapped around her shoulders for support. Coach's body was dwindling, his posture was painfully arched, and his beard had turned entirely grey. The most youthful thing on his body was his amiable smile. Coach has only endured over ten years of actual living. His physical body has aged 90 odd years, but he has saved immeasurable lifetimes for mankind. Coach was a riddle, all the way until his finale. The Earth's 'knight in shining armor' paused once he reached the entranceway to the plane's cabin. There were displays of maps dangling from the wall in front of Coach. He signaled to them before he was finished being ushered to his seat.

Technology had become so advanced there was rarely a need for paper maps anymore. Heck, paper anything. Coach had lived through the era of inevitable technological transitions into societal customs. It was now the norm to have high powered, and addictive, devices as an extra appendage. But for all the access to information, and digitally socialized realms, people were becoming oblivious to the things that matter. The age of verbal communication had started its degradation. Humans were actively besieged by legions of misinformation and nonsense. There was an artificial essence capturing hold of humanity's biological ways.

The most worrisome facet of the advancing tech was its negative correlation to humanity's environmental indifference towards this most recent, and narrowly escaped, disaster. This same type of mortal apathy ultimately led to the fatal breakdown of Earth's atmosphere. Alas, humans ignorantly resumed their lack of concern for Mother Nature. People and corporations felt they were again invincible to a climate change apocalypse or any other natural catastrophe. They proceeded in their careless methods, excessively ravaging this new, Coach-derived, Earth as if nothing alarming had happened. Humanity believed that the American government had the remedies, or the power, to create any cures to combat another crisis. What a naïve species we have become.

Mother Nature is an intricate and perishable system of organically working parts. She is a fickle beast, though. The Mother of our Nature will adapt to its conditions. She will evolve through her circumstances. She will naturally battle to survive like any other living organism in her kingdom. She will continue to combat the increasingly adverse effects that the human virus has had on Earth's life expectancy.

Chapter 29:

Jessica picked up her phone while getting seated on the plane, "Hello, what's the good word?!" it was her father, Vick.

"The boys in the lab got a partial match on Coach's DNA..." Victor turned away from the phone to answer a question from someone nearby. "...Sorry about that, Jess. They are saying that he has traces of Picea

Rubens. Red spruce or some coniferous genetics!" Victor finished

emphatically relaying the message to Jess.

"What do you mean!? Coach is part tree?!" Jessica was astonished

by the news. She glanced over at Coach's weary smile. It made perfect

sense to her.

"Yes. He is more tree than human. But the Doc told me it was a

harmonious fusion of plant and human DNA. They have never seen this shit

before, Jess!" Victor replied to her daughter with a reciprocally shocked

tone. It did not make perfect sense to Victor, but he decided not to fret after

all Coach has sacrificed.

"That makes so much sense, though, Dad! All that brilliant nature he

can conjure from within! I knew my Coach was of a new breed!" Jessica

felt a delightful rush, like she had finally deciphered the riddle.

Victor laughed at his descendant's enthusiasm and retorted, "He is

the first of his kind... As far as we know."

"I don't think I will ever love another being as much as I love

Coach. I have to go though. We are taking off momentarily. Thanks for the update! I will see you later." Jessica confessed her heart to Victor before terminating the call.

Coach was sitting next to the window and smiling as the sun beat down on his unkempt face. The steward of the plane consulted with Jessica about where their destination was to be. The sweet smell of vanilla and sugar came wafting through the pressurized air as the flight attendant was gracefully striding about the cabin. Victor had requested that the flight crew prepare waffles and fruit for Coach, out of respect and admiration. Mr. Fasser remembered on the first morning he met Coach, just a couple days ago, how much he enjoyed that breakfast Sofia made. It was his charming effort to portray respect to such a remarkable entity.

Jessica pulled out her phone and a map of the North America. She urged Coach to pick a spot he would like to visit before he succumbs to his mysterious conclusion. Jessie figured that he has only experienced two areas of this extensive world. Perhaps, he would like to go somewhere exotic. The smell of waffles enticed Coach's smiley arch just a bit deeper. Coach did not even glance at the map when he planted his wizened finger on one spot, The Smoky Mountains. Only a small portion of The Smokies had been afflicted by the pervasive death fires.

"You want to go to the Smoky Mountains, Coach?!" Jessica rhetorically stated for her affirmation. Coach just continued smiling. "Then, that's where we shall go, Sweet Coach."

The pilot was informed of Coach's desired destination, the plane ascended from the runway, and Coach was served his merited stack of waffles once they were airborne. It was the minimum that humans could do for their environmental champion. The plane ride was short, and the pilot maneuvered the stealthy aircraft to land as close to Coach's indicated location as he could. It was a familiar sight for Coach, except for intermittent portions of the blackened forest. This was Roger's property, where he had 'grown-up'.

"We are here, Coach! I hope this is where you meant." Jessica informed Coach, and she helped his brittle body from his cushioned seat.

Coach smiled while he gently made his way to his birthland. This region was a few miles from the exact area he was hybridized by that special spruce in Coach's Valley. But Roger and Coach spent so many days searching through these woodlands that Coach instantaneously regained his

bearings. Coach pointed to the Northeastern region of a specific mountain.

He signaled to where he reminisced that Roger's stone house was located.

"Coach, that is quite a hike. Do you think you will be alright?!"

Jessica asked the invulnerable Coach, hoping to squeak out a word still.

Coach beamed at Jessie. He appeared nimbler at this moment, his feet were

bare per usual, and Coach was incrementally invigorated on his intimate

territory.

"Well, the sun is going down soon... We better get to hiking."

Jessica endorsed her best friend's reaction, locked arms with him, and let

Coach lead the way.

It was a two-hour trek through Roger's colossal acreage and up the

side of the mountain. Coach lost his footing and balance several times along

the way, but his determination never wavered. Coach's confidant aided

where she could, but Coach was feverishly leading this excursion. He was

being compelled by one last surge of natural mystic.

The two explorers scaled this parcel of the mountain until they

stumbled upon a remote property. Paula had informed Jessica of Coach's time with Roger, and the connection these two had when Coach was in child form. This home appeared desolate, though, and Jessie recalled Roger's age being in the seventies at that previous time.

"Coach, I don't think Roger is here anymore." Jessica declared this to soothe Coach's wandering eyes.

The sun was leisurely setting across from their current mountainside view. The wind was firmly gusting west towards the sinking sun. It was abnormally stronger than Coach ever remembered. The foliage on the trees shivered and quaked, making beautiful natural melodies. It was as if the surrounding nature of this land was welcoming their estranged brother back home.

From inside the shadowed porch came an accent, "Is that ma' boy?! Coach?!" It was Roger's hoarse voice inquiring from inside his obscure dwelling.

"C'mon and let me get a look at ye, Coach." Roger delicately opened the screened porch door with his hand-crafted cane and delicately paced his way towards his wunderkind. Ole Rog was flabbergasted at Coach's crumpled state. It was like looking in the mirror.

"Hello, Roger. I'm Jessica, Coach's best friend. It is a pleasure to meet the man that found this miracle finally." Jess greeted Roger and bypassed the formal handshake for a hug.

"Pleasure to meet ye, Missy." Ole Rog basked in the warm embrace of another human.

He turned over to his smiling and withering companion, Coach, and made a crude joke, "She musta sucked the life outta ye, eh, Ole Boy?" Ole Rog apologized after saying it aloud, but Jessica was not offended. She had an objective sense of humor and character throughout her life. Coach was an essential influence in that.

Jessie had snickered at Ole Rog before she said, "That was a good one... Coach pointed to this area on a map. This is where he wanted to conclude his journey. Coach saved us all from certain death!"

Ole Rog continued to examine Coach's accelerated maturation. He could not look away from his friend's smile. "I reckoned it was this here, Coach that settled that mess. Always knew he had a grander destiny than stayin' on this mountain with my old ass." Ole Rog's eyes were laden with admiration, and they overflowed.

As Ole Rog did his best to hold back his tears of reverence. He bluntly demanded, "Tell me everythin' ye can 'bout Coach's journey." Jessica Fasser sat with Coach and Ole Rog on a bench in front of the stone house. She revealed, to Ole Rog, every bit of story she could recall.

Chapter 30:

Elsewhere around the world, chaos was being reigned in. Humanity was temporarily resuscitated. Paula called on the comfort of Frank during these troubling times, and he was prompt in his response. The two eventually formed a domestic union and shared life's blessings. Frank and Paula would be forever relieved of the anguish for their lost loved ones, except for their Coach. But they could bolster and rejoice in his splendid memory, together. Karen and Victor readjusted their lives after resolving this mortally appalling dilemma. They both desired to spend more time together and cherish their limited period on this Earth. Sofia eventually started a family of her own, and the Fasser's succored them as kin. Jessie Fasser would become a renowned environmental biologist. She would win multiple Nobel Peace Prizes throughout her career. Jessica won these distinguished prizes for her role in facilitating eco-friendly, and progressive, industrial innovations. Jessie would dedicate every prize she achieved to the Earth's true hero, Coach.

The sun was now in its glossy terminus of setting back at the bench where Coach, Ole Rog, and Jess were reminiscing. Well, Ole Rog and Jessica were. Coach was smiling, though, and they all ogled at the horizon, erupting with a medley of dazzling pigments.

"This is the most beautiful sunset I have ever seen, Coach!" Jessica thrillingly shouted next to her. Where Coach was lifeless at the end of the bench, Jessica's eyes were waterlogged, she could sense that Coach had slipped away.

"I think he is-" Jessica desperately spoke towards Roger.

Ole Rog abruptly interjected, "-Ye Suga', I think he is too." Roger's eyes were swamped. He welcomed Coach into this world. Now, Ole Rog will be here to witness Coach's departure from it.

"I suppose that the circle of life," Ole Roger pronounced to the suffering Jessica. Roger placed his arm around her in comfort. The two had their heads slumped down as they harmoniously wept together.

Coach's heart had stopped beating, his eyes were now closed, but his smile stayed behind. As Coach's dear friends were mourning over his physical expiration, his body persisted in its decay. In a matter of fifty seconds, Coach's fleshy cadaver turned into a swirl of turquoise vapor. The swirl consisted of ashy particles and premature, turquoise gem-cones. There were six, two-inch-long, exotically lustrous gem-cones floating in the atomized cloud of Coach's relics. The wind speeds became more turbulent as Coach disintegrated. Mother Nature was guiding Coach's leftovers as she had steered him through his Earthly journey.

"What is happening!?" Jessica yelled to Ole Rog over the hectically whooshing gusts.

Ole Rog tried his best speculation, "I reckon Coach is preparin' to spread his seeds!" Roger pointed toward the multiple, and radiant, turquoise stars churning in the tornado of blueish ash next to Jess.

The subsequent flurry of airstreams charged into Coach's residual cloud and dispersed his reproductive kernels in several directions. Most were perched in nearby areas where the land had yet to be restored. Each gem-cone had spread on a distinct path, all within a ten-mile radius of where Ole Rog and Jess still lingered. The traveled seeds hastily burrowed into whatever ground they landed on in this National Forest district. Both Roger and Jessica halted their crying once Coach's final act concluded. The natural squalls subsided, and the forest calmed all around them as if it just took a sigh of relief. It was one last, and appropriately mysterious, display from their companion.

"How would you explain that then, Roger?!" Jessica probed Roger, hoping he had more perspective than her absolute bemusement.

Ole Rog took his time before responding. He genuinely sought to provide the best insight he could for Jessica in these tender moments. "Well, I reckon Coach just kept whatever he was, survivin'. Passin' on to the next generations... " Roger continued his theory "... From that magical story ye done told me. It sounds like Coach was created to make sure nature don't die. And who destroyin' this Earth and nature?" He questioned Jessica to see if she was following his train of thought.

"Humans." Jessie answered, well aware of humanity's negligent practices.

"Yessum. And it looks like nature want to keep on livin'." Ole Rog concisely assessed his experiences combined with Jessica's sagas of Coach.

"So, you think there will be more Coaches to come?" Jessie's curiosity was mounting when she replied with this question.

"Sweetheart, the way I seen 'civilization' treat this here Earth. I would count on it," Roger openly stated.

Jessica had an amused face on when she maintained her line of investigation, "I saw six of those glowing pods in that cloud! I am assuming those are Coach's seeds?!"

"Well, I reckon that be a good guess." Ole Rog was assured in his response.

Jessica frantically rustled after her possessions, preparing to go search for the gem-cones this instant.

"What do ye think ye doin', Missy?!" Roger firmly questioned Jessica after observing her frenetic movements. Ole Rog grasped that Coach was an initial, and critical, element in the evolution of Mother Nature's subsistence. He had no intentions of impeding the natural order of nature.

"We gotta go... Or I am gonna go… Gather Coach's seeds!" Jessica pronounced and started for the door before Roger shouted at her backside.

"Ye best stop ye pacin' 'bout!! Is nighttime now, what do ye plan to do wit the seeds anyhow?!" Roger retorted with a legitimate query.

Jessie rashly flung her bag to the floor out of protest, and countered, "I am going get the damn seeds! Coach's progeny deserves to be nurtured and properly cared for!" she was pouting like a teenager.

"We best leave nature to do what nature do! It made Coach. She'll make mo' Coaches if that what she meant to do." Ole Rog shared his sentiments about natural selection. He genuinely believed that nature would see that more Coaches were made if that's what this Earth needs.

While reality sunk Jessica into the nearest chair. Ole Rog resumed his harsh wisdom "... Hell, maybe humans the virus. The Earth done made one creature, like Coach... Ta' save the environment. Maybe Earth jus' made six mo'. Make sure it never happen 'gain?!"

"... I never forgot 'bout Coach's kinfolk. They disappear in that janky forest... " Ole Rog trailed his head to the side as he ruminated. "... Well, them Coach seeds gone be here anytime ye wanna visit."

Roger insisted that Jessica spend the night, for it was too dark to hike back at this hour. Jessica and Roger sat around the dinner table grazing and recalling the triumphs of Coach at 9:37 pm on February 3rd, 2008. The expiry date of their dear comrade, counsel, confidant, savior, kid, and inspiration. Their Coach.

The morning of February 4th brought on a different feel to the Earth's ambiance. Perhaps because it was the first morning sprung without Coach in ten years. Throughout the previous night, Coach's distributed gem-cones had delved into their respective grounds. Shortly after, tree saplings sprouted from each nestled cone. From dusk until dawn, these six turquoise cones phenomenally transformed into enchantingly golden-trunked, red spruce trees. Each tree had soared above 100 feet. Their leaves were an exceptional purple color, and buds of deep crimson pinecones formed at the ends of sporadic branches. But between particular bifurcations and along the golden trunk of the tree, turquoise specks glimmered. There were dozens of these turquoise particles on each tree. Here is where these pupil gem-cones would mature until Mother Nature deems it essential to hypnotize and hybridize more human subjects.

Through the light of day, Jessica and Roger could see the developed golden spruces. They were spread throughout their various locations, but each was visible from the front of Roger's property. The shimmer that the trees reflected reminded them both of Coach's smile.

"Ye can come to visit any a them trees ye see out there. Any time ye want." Ole Rog gestured this welcoming offer.

Ole Rog walked with Jessica as far as he could make it on the property these days. Jessie thanked Roger for the hospitality and comradery before returning to her life.

"Well, sun come up! I reckon I be joinin' ye soon, Ole Coach." Roger decreed aloud, to himself, as he struggled to hike back up the mountainside. Ole Rog peacefully died in his sleep, three days later, at the ripe age of eighty-four. His body remains entombed in his secluded stone house, watching over the future generations of Coach.

Not even two months later, and the human species had reverted to its haphazard behaviors. An abundance of individuals changed their tactics in their daily routines out of the newfound respect for their environment. But the greed of man is too profoundly rooted in the mercantile structure that rules over civilization. The human culture degenerated back to the "profit above everything" mentality. Conglomerates and tycoons took a staggeringly brief reprieve, from the spoiling of the Earth, while the crisis was in full swing. But once the chaos simmered down, it was back to the status quo. Industrial runoff flowed into our waterways again, Coach's greenery was commercialized, and natural resources were transplanted from below the surface with toxic derivatives... This terrestrial treachery perpetuated as it had for decades. Thankfully, Mother Nature had prepared for such duplicity.

Chapter 31:

On the open road, cruising through Tennessee's portion of Interstate 40, a caravan of friends were on an adventure to an unfamiliar national park. It was nearing the end of summer in 2008. There were four couples, two of which were pregnant, and three children in this convoy driving through The Great Smoky Mountains. This parade had toured from Arizona and then through the American south. The Appalachian Mountains were the last site on their nature-inspired expedition. They had originally planned to see the northern trails, but some ecological intuition was leading the motorcade to an exclusive spot. Three cars deep with the team's captain, Stevie, at the head of the rolling series. Stevie had not consulted a map since they crossed into the national park district. He was being steered by a silent partner. The vehicles spiraled down a dangerous stretch of road, and fellow passengers felt unnerved.

"Where is Steve going?!" One couple in another car discussed.

The parade had landed in a green wonderland. There was ample room for all the cars to park. The sign in the bay area read Coach's Valley. The children squealed with joy, the parents hooted in astonishment, and the air was intoxicating. Variations of 'amazing' and 'incredible' were being exchanged between the merged group. They each grabbed their corresponding gear as rapidly as they could. They were all itching to explore this magical forest. Stevie led the pack onto the inviting trail that started the hike from Coach's Valley. None could find Coach's Valley on their maps or phones, but no one looked that hard either. It was a mesmerizing place.

Time felt like it had stopped during the journey. The party of eleven (and two halves) were all inebriated with supreme euphoria. There was only bulging eyes and howls of pleasant sensations throughout the assembly of friends. They had been walking for what felt like two hours, but not one member of the party complained. Upon entering a distinctly unique section of this forest, one child spotted a radiant turquoise treasure. The turquoise gem-cone rested on the grassy meadow near the base of a sublimely golden trunk.

"Hey! What's that!?" one child yelled and ran towards the foreign object.

Stevie felt an alarming chill stretch down his spine. He vehemently surveyed around to gather the area. None of the team's technological devices were accessible in this peculiar region. Stevie could not determine where the trail back was any longer. It was as if it vanished once the entire group entered this zone. As the rest of the group was still in awe by the splendor of this gorgeous parcel, Stevie felt panic set in.

Little Timmy shrieked sounds of horror, "Mommy! It burns!" The turquoise gem-cone had begun its amalgamation into the boy's frame.

Sounds of bliss quickly turned into screeches of dread. Steven saw each individual magnetized to one of the dozen turquoise nuggets scattered across the forest's floor. There was nowhere for them to escape. Stevie spun around in a circle, listening to each one of his friend's squeals of agony as their bodies commenced disintegration. It was only a matter of seconds before Stevie eventually surrendered to the allure of the closest turquoise gem-cone. He would be one of many sacrifices for the greater good of life. Humanity has forced Mother Nature to utilize cruelty as kindness. She will endure the ignorance of man. She will outlast.

The End.

CPSIA information can be obtained
at www.ICGtesting.com
Printed in the USA
LVHW042022121220
674002LV00002B/78